Wait Till the Sun Shines, Nellie

Wait Till

a novel by Audrey Gellen Maas

the Sun Shines, Nellie

The New American Library NAL

c.1

Published by The New American Library, Inc.
1301 Avenue of the Americas, New York, New York 10019

Published simultaneously in Canada by
General Publishing Company, Ltd.

Library of Congress Catalog Card Number: 66-26048

Printed in the United States of America

For Peter

Wait Till the Sun Shines, Nellie

Five of her admirers tell the whole paradoxical tragicomic story of Nellie a delightful exuberant, sexy, emotional girl who lives life with zeal and yet commits suicide at the age of twenty-two.

The Painter

The police were the ones who called to tell me about Nellie and how she tried to kill herself. They told me to come down to Roosevelt Hospital because there had been an "accident," and the victim of the accident had said to call me because I would know what to do if she died and if she didn't. When I got to Roosevelt, she was dead.

The police asked me to identify the body, and of course they questioned me as to what and who I was. They asked what my relationship to the girl was. They were very proper police, and wondered why I, a married man, should be the only person this young woman would call upon in a case of this nature. I said I was her friend. It was very complicated—that whole business with the police—and I don't like to think about it.

After they had finished with me, I went home and didn't sleep and waited for the morning papers to read

1

what the papers would say about this girl, this Nellie, who had killed herself.

When you read about a suicide in the newspapers, it takes on a very abstract quality. You wonder why the person did it. You wonder what the proverbial straw was, and why you can't do it yourself. You look at the picture of the person—if there is a picture. In Nellie's case there was.

I made an imaginary collage of that picture in the paper and the one in my mind's eye, the one of the dead Nellie whose head, as always, was tilted a little to the right. A poseur, even in death.

I met her on a Sunday.

I had taken a studio uptown in one of those old buildings near Columbia University. It had been built in the days of eleven-room apartments when rooms were rooms and ceilings were on the top of great walls. Now the apartments were torn up and broken down, but the ceilings had stayed the same and so had the windows and the light. I don't know whether or not the apartment was my excuse to get away from a wife who I thought was stifling my creative impulse or whether it was an excuse to pretend that I had a creative impulse to stifle, but it was a studio and you really can't be or pretend to be a painter without a studio.

Nellie always said it was half studio, half *"pied-à-terre."* She explained what *"pied-à-terre"* meant in French, and why all men in France had *"pied-à-terres"* whether or not they could or could not paint.

My wife hated France. Not that she preferred Italy. There are people that say, "I can't stand France, especially Paris, it's cold and cruel and ruthless and just like New York, but Italy. . . ." There are people that say that, but not my wife. She hated Italy just as much as France.

2

Each day I would go to the studio and sit and look across the river at the Palisades Amusement Park and try to paint . . . and one evening, just about the time they turn on all the neon signs a girl rang my bell and said, "I'm terribly sorry to bother you, Mr. Isaacs, but it's Sunday and I can't buy a bottle of liquor and they won't serve me at any of the bars around here, and I really need a drink. And I guessed that you, being a painter and having all those empty liquor bottles in your garbage can—not that I go through your garbage cans and count them—you would have one. A drink I mean."

That was Nellie.

She explained in great detail the liquor laws of New York State. "You can't get a drink unless you can prove you're over eighteen or unless you know someone. You know what I mean? And I really don't know anyone around here that well yet and I don't have any proof of age. I mean, who carries around a birth certificate? And I can't drive and I've lost my draft card.

"They won't believe me that I'm over eighteen, or else they *say* they don't because they don't want me hanging around, and the funny thing is that I don't want to hang around—I just want to belt and run. I'm really way over eighteen, though, isn't that the damndest thing?"

She didn't look way over eighteen. . . . She looked like a hoyden child, trembling with outrage, not so much at not getting what she wanted, but at not getting what she was entitled to. She looked like a ragamuffin with high fever. . . . One of the Hundred Neediest, needing a drink. . . . All eyes, sweet mouth and long, long hair, full of moving outraged hands *Allegro, Vibrato, Vivace con molto.* Life, vitality. . . .

I asked her if she preferred France to Italy and she said she adored both but hadn't been to either yet, and then she said that she hadn't just come in off the street, that

3

she was my neighbor and she lived upstairs. She said that
you could be neighbors just as well living upstairs as
next-door and that whenever she walked downstairs she
passed my garbage and that's how she knew I'd have a
drink because of all my empty liquor bottles. She said
that she knew that she and I would eventually become
friends sooner or later, with or without the liquor, because she liked the looks of my garbage. She told me that
she could tell that I had character because I separated
the organic garbage from the papers and bottles, and because she knew just from the nonorganic garbage that I
was a painter.

"Guess how I knew? Guess and I'll tell you."

I told her I couldn't guess and she told me it was because of my brush rags.

"You have the most beautiful colors on your brush
rags. I always see them in the garbage can. They're all my
colors, and you can't have those kind of rags and that
many liquor bottles and not come up with a painter."

I invited her in and invited her to sit down and she
sat down with a grace and elegance I guess they teach
at dancing school, and then she started to laugh and said,
"Hey, now I know somebody—so I can get a drink on
Sunday."

I asked her what her preference was and she said it
was bourbon. I poured her one on the rocks which she
explained was best with a twist of lemon peel and could
she have two pieces of lemon peel. She told me that
lemon peel was on its way out, but that she loved to mar-
inate it in the bourbon and then eat it. She bolted the
bourbon and ate the lemon peel in the style of Charles
Chaplin when he sucked the meat off every hobnail on
that shoe in *The Gold Rush*. And after she finished her
lemon peel she held out her glass and said, *"Bis, bis—*

4

that's French. It means could I have another? Because the last one was so good."

I made her another and I made one for myself and put two pieces of lemon peel in each and lighted a cigarette, and she asked if she could have one, too. She said, "Boy, I'm really Minnie the Moocher, aren't I? Am I not? I know that 'am I not' is correct usage but it sounds like you're asking *if* you are rather than *what* you are. And I'm very sure that I *am*, but not sure *what* I am, and please now can I have a light?"

I took the cigarette from her hand and put it in my mouth, lighted it, handed it back. She took a drag, let half the smoke slip out from between her lips, and then she held that cigarette between her thumb and her forefinger and cracked it out in an ashtray, and she said, "I get so bored with smoking, just after one drag. . . . But I'll probably ask to bum another in about seven minutes. . . .

"It's one of my most significant syndromes, and I've read that Tallulah had the same thing about cigs that I do. I think it signifies a low threshold of satisfaction with the immediate, *n'est-ce pas?* And I have a voluminous appetite."

She said, "Is voluminous the right word? Or should I have used insatiable?"

I just laughed.

"I think I'm satiable. I think I'm eminently satiable."

I should have finished my drink and told her it was time for me to go home. It was. But I didn't want to go home, and I didn't want to tell her that I had to. I sat down, and there we were, me and Nellie and the beginning of a beautiful friendship. There we were smokin' and drinkin' and smokin'. She was the one who said it. She said, "Here we are smokin' and drinkin', drinkin' and smokin' just like W. C. Fields. Do you ever go to his movies?"

I said I used to go but I hadn't gone for a long time, and she told me that they played all the time right down at the New Yorker Theatre on Eighty-eighth Street, and that "smokin' and drinkin', drinkin' and smokin'" came from *The Bank Dick*—where his mother-in-law used to say it through clenched teeth, and then she said, "Maybe we could go sometime?"

And I told her I was married.

She said, "Then maybe we could go in the afternoon?"

I guess I must have given her a blank stare because she said, "I'm a pragmatist, a satiable pragmatist." I said, "So am I." And then I realized that for the first time in a long time I was having a good time. And I sat back and enjoyed it.

People say that New York is full of girls like Nellie, that you see them everywhere. I had seen girls, but none like Nellie. To me she was unique and delicious, and she lived upstairs and she was sitting opposite me drinking my bourbon and eating all my lemon peel. *Rara avis*, a strange and wondrous bird, who told the truth because it was pragmatic.

We talked.

She had come to New York—she didn't say from where —to go to Barnard College and things hadn't exactly worked out there but she had met a very nice boy who worked in the Administration Building. She said he was a male secretary and she added that that told you a lot about Barnard and a lot about him. The very nice boy had gotten her a lot of very nice forms which she very nicely filled out and sent back home, and God knows how, but she convinced her parents that she was doing brilliantly in school and they kept sending her money while she was working on her true calling, which was becom-

6

ing a nightclub singer. She told me that she sent home terrific marks and that her parents were very proud of her and they'd be even prouder when she was a star. She said she firmly believed that she had a great career in the making. She said her theme song was "Wait Till the Sun Shines, Nellie," which was the saddest song in the world, and her style was based on her two favorites, Helen Morgan and Ruth Etting, because they were both sad and she herself was inherently sad. And when she used the word "inherently" it was with great pride. She said she studied *Thirty Days to a More Powerful Vocabulary* in order to pass the College Boards and had come out in the best percentile and that she kept up on her vocabulary because that was part of her parents' thinking she was studying.

She said, "God, I write the phoniest letters. But anyway, it won't matter after I'm successful. At least to me. Because I'd rather be W. C. Fields than Phi Beta Kappa. You know what I mean?"

And I knew that you had to keep from laughing when you listened to Nellie because all of her plans and pronouncements were made with such a sense of sobriety that you couldn't tell her they were sophomoric.

She wasn't old enough to be a sophomore.

She asked me if I liked the people in the building, and I told her that I didn't know them and she said that they were all lousy, that she knew them through the washing machines.

"I go down to the basement," she said, "to wash out my things and it's like Transylvania there. Boy, do they give me the evil eye and I don't even deserve it. They think I'm lazy because I do my underwear in the machine instead of by hand and I feel like telling them that's what washing machines were invented for, you know, to wash things!"

7

And she shrugged as if it were a hopeless case and it was too bad that she couldn't reform the laundry room. And then she laughed and said, "That's why I was so fascinated by the idea of you, a single man in the building. Not that you're really single. I know that now. But when you're *here* you're single and I'm really a man's woman. I relate best to men."

I said I was glad.

She told me that it was obvious that I must have marital problems. And when I asked why she said, "Why is because of the studio, and you staying here now when you should go home. You know a *'pied-à-terre'* means a foot in the soil in French, literally, and it means figuratively just what it is, a place away from your wife. It means that you don't feel at home on your home ground, so you try to dig in elsewhere. Right? It means you pretend to live where you don't really live and you're too scared to live where you pretend you live. But now I'm here, and I'm going to help you. Help you live."

She reminded me of all the things I had lost and hoped for and counted on and wanted to be and see, and she reminded me of the love affairs that I had never had and the few women I'd always wanted and been afraid to have.

So she lured me into a devil's bargain. Sometimes I think I might have suggested it anyway, but in my heart I know it was all really Nellie's idea.

The idea was that I should paint her portrait.

Should I have said that to capture the essence of a human being—that exquisite essence that is essential to a painting, if it be a portrait—was something I had never dared attempt? Should I have said that I had parlayed my talent into a talent for lucrative marriages, that all my shows went by the boards as "representative of the current trend?"

8

Should I have said, "I can't paint you because I can't paint?"

Should or shouldn't—I didn't.

Nellie said that all great performers had their portraits painted, and assuming her immortality was inevitable why should she not be immortalized beforehand rather than after? It was convenient, logical, and she could make some money. I hadn't counted on paying her but she said it would be very helpful and that I could paint her nude. She said, "I've got this great thing. It's a space between my rib cage that I think you'll really like. It's supposed to be bad for your stomach muscles, but I think it's gorgeous."

She stopped for a moment and then looked down at herself and she said, "You know, I like my body."

I didn't say, "So do I," or "How nice." I just said, "How much do I have to pay you?"

"A dollar and a half an hour and all I can drink."

"Hours?"

"At my convenience."

I said, "No deal."

"I'll provide lunch and I'll work nine to five."

"I don't work nine to five."

"Eleven to six?"

"How can a painter work like a male secretary?"

"Listen," she said, "even Eisenhower painted!"

And having been put in my place, I didn't answer. So she said, "I'll work whenever you want. I'm scale and avail—that's a show-business term that means you're very inexpensive and always looking for work. And let's not haggle any more because it'll be fun for both of us and I bet it'll be a great picture, so it'll be worth your while. Tell you what. You just take a broom and knock on the ceiling in the morning when you're ready for me, and I'll come down. *N'est-ce pas?*"

I agreed and we had another drink and I said that we were both drunk and she said we should both go home and then I saw a tilt of a head that made a face turn toward you and away at the same time, and an almost orgiastically mingled look of pleasure and pain and she said, "Even though I'll let you do me naked I'm not going to sleep with you." And I said, "It's polite to wait to be asked."

She walked to the door and she opened it a crack and slithered out and then she stuck her head back inside and said, "I've always wanted to know an older man and now I do. . . . I'm glad it's you!"

I listened to her lurch up the stairs and close her door. I heard her footsteps on the ceiling, and decided to walk home. I walked down Broadway with its garbage, and garbage-pail pickers and its *abogados* and barbecued chickens and seamless hose on sale, and I listened to the benchsitters with the no-good daughters-in-law, and looked at the chairsitters who gave you the privilege of a peek between their legs, and waved to all the Riker's junkies, and I remembered when they got a "most-wanted murderer" in a hotel off 104th Street, and I wondered why I went to the movies or made sandwiches instead of painting, and I crossed the park and wondered why I didn't like my current wife. Maybe because she didn't talk and she didn't want to sing, and she didn't have a space between her rib cage and she didn't like France, much less Italy, and Nellie did. Nellie did everything. Nellie loved Nellie's body.

I walked down Fifth and across to Madison and halfway to Park and thought how nice it would be if my kids went to P.S. 6 instead of a private school.

And when I was fumbling for my keys which my wife said I always lost because I didn't want to come home, I thought of my upstairs neighbor and surreptitiously the background music returned and those few hours in the studio seemed like "21," the way you imagined it should be, or Roseland when no one's there and just a few people are dancing, under water, and just looking at each other; or like the Ideal Bar and Grill where nobody asks any questions and nobody tells any lies.

And I thought of all the things I should have painted on the days when I didn't paint, and then I remembered that Nellie hadn't asked to look at my paintings and that I hadn't asked her to sing. Maybe because we were both very lonesome and grateful enough to have someone to talk to without having to make judgments. She accepted the fact that I was a real painter and I accepted the fact that she was a real singer. And we had both made plans for a project for immortality believing in each other's ability to execute and be executed.

I lay awake all night wondering whether or not she would show up.

Next morning I fled to the studio and looked at all the names next to the doorbells. Her name wasn't written next to any of the bells. I ran upstairs and grabbed a broom and pounded on the ceiling. I listened and then I heard her walking around up there, and I heard her open her door and close it and walk down the stairs very slowly.

I felt like a blind man at the movies until she opened my door and said, "I'm not ready."

She was wearing a salmon-pink kimono, and she had a paper bag in her hand. She told me that it was her Vanity Kit because she didn't have any Vanity and asked where the bathroom was. She explained that she hadn't yet done her toilette and that for this painting, not that she had posed for any others, for this painting she was going

11

to rub her entire body with Elizabeth Arden Body Lotion because it gave you a flesh-toned glow. She told me that she would start preparing herself and I should start preparing my palette and that she didn't drink coffee because it was bad for your nerves but that when she was greased and ready could she have a beer?

I had a canvas stretched for a painting I had never done. But the canvas was right for Nellie because it was long and narrow, and so was she.

I set it on an easel and started going through my paints. And then she hollered out from the bathroom, "You know what I dreamed last night? I dreamed that I was married to you! And it was awful! And then I got pregnant by George Raft, sleazy old-timey George Raft, and I felt so terrible because he's so recognizable that you would have known right away the baby wasn't yours. . . . Can you imagine a little baby flipping a coin? I saw that on *The Late Show*. He really did it. It was his bit. George Raft's, I mean, not the baby's." And then she came out of the bathroom.

And she said, "Christ, I can't remember how she stands." When I asked her "Who?" she said, "Simonetta Vespucci, of course. People tell me I remind them of her. She had a body like me. Narrow shoulders and. . . ."

"And the rib cage."

She laughed, "Yes—the rib cage, and hair like me. . . . Simonetta Vespucci. Venus on the Half Shell. Botticelli's Venus."

"I know."

"That's how I want you to do me. . . . I don't mean rising from the sea, or on a shell, or anything like that but you know, just the general floating idea. You don't have to have water to float. . . . It would be kind of nice, wouldn't it? I mean, if we're going for immortality, let's go all the way."

12

I said, *"D'accord,"* and she said, "That means Okay in French, right?"

I said, "Right."

"Where should I stand?"

"Over there."

She walked in that direction like an Indian casing the woods, and then she found a spot, and turned toward me and let the robe slide down that Elizabeth-Ardened-Flesh-toned flesh.

She did indeed have a space between her rib cage and narrow shoulders. She stood on tip-toe holding her arms outstretched, and she asked if she looked like she was floating. I told her just to stand straight and still, because she'd never be able to hold that ridiculous pose for more than thirty seconds, and besides, she looked more like the Winged Victory than Venus.

I started to mix colors and she asked why I wasn't going to do sketches first and wasn't it dangerous to start right on the canvas, and I told her not to talk and she said, "Never?" and I told her she could talk during the breaks.

She obeyed and stood motionless, elegant and haughty, immortal in her own imagination. That lasted for about a minute and a half and then the hauteur disappeared and she just stood there—absolutely still. I had never seen anyone stand quite so perfectly still in my life.

Once I asked her how she did it and she said that she did it Yoga-style. "I say to myself: toe be still, toe be still, foot be still, foot be still, ankle be still, ankle, shin, knee . . . it requires gorgeous concentration and purifies my mind. It's as if I'm working just as hard as you are, you know, for the painting, and for Immortality."

I never gave Nellie that painting. I thought of it as mine alone. Not at first, of course. Only later. After she left.

13

• • •

The first morning was wonderful. The fear that I would never start much less finish never even came. It was inevitable, golden and easy, and I looked at Nellie and the painting and at myself with the schizophrenic eye of someone who says, "Well, how do you like that guy?" about himself.

Her naked body was no longer a body, but a series of images. Not a unity but an amalgamation—chopped up into singular and unique sections and segments. Only the face was whole and one with itself. I was painting, painting in a trance. I was dancing under water and she was floating, and then she asked if she could have that beer I had promised her and I looked up and all the segments of her body fell together like one of those magnetic toys, and I looked at her altogether and she wrapped the robe around her like a sarong and said, "Holy Mother of God, I bet it's been an hour and it'll be all your fault if I die of thirst!"

I got a beer for her and one for me and told her she could rest. There was as much movement and vibrancy in her voice and eyes and hands and body as there had been stillness in the stance.

Whenever I told her the break had been long enough she'd say in an English accent, "Shall I assume my stance. Then, what?"

We both thought it was terribly funny. I can't remember why.

We would always talk "in depth" during our breaks. Nellie would choose the subject and set the tone.

She would start by saying, "Tell me about painting! I only know a little. Didn't it all begin with the cavemen in the caves at the Alamo?"

And I would say that it began with the cavemen in the

14

caves at Altamira, or maybe before, so she said, "Oh, yes, the Alamo was Pearl Harbor, you know, 'Let's remember Pearl Harbor as we did the Alamo-o!' "

And she said, "You know, I wish I'd been alive when it was really fashionable to be a Communist."

I told her that in some circles it still was. She told me that she loved Bosch and Breughel but that she didn't know one from the other and I told her that it really didn't matter as long as she loved both of them.

She said that she had once read a book by a man named Dalton Trumbo called *Johnny Got His Gun* and the man—Johnny—had lost everything in the war and he was just a trunk who couldn't talk or listen or see or anything . . . but he could eventually communicate, which was the point of the book, and that it was terrific that painters could communicate just by painting, and did I know what I was going to communicate in my portrait of her?

She said, "It's funny, but I've never known a painter before, and I've always wanted to know one because I want to know what makes someone think they can be a painter. I once tried—and I thought I was awful. But for all I know, maybe I was good. Look at Van Gogh. He got put down by everybody but he was the best."

She told me that the only way to cook bay scallops was with chives and shallot and the only way to serve tomatoes was with dill and that all the early American whalers drank beer and ale for breakfast and could she have another one.

I remember when I handed her the second beer she reached out to take it and the robe slid down, and I could see all of one breast and half the other, and it was much more exciting than when she'd been totally naked. She drank the beer right out of the can, and I remember

15

that I wished I were Frans Hals and could capture utter vulgarity combined with sweet delicacy, and I remember that I remembered I was forty-eight with one coronary for openers, and that she was pretending that I was Botticelli and she was Venus. So I told her that the break was over and that I'd like to begin again.

Around twelve-thirty she asked me if I were hungry, and I was, so she said that she'd make lunch if I'd make drinks. She said that lunch would be *"à la vie bohème"* which would fit in with *"pied-à-terre."*

She put the kimono on correctly and walked upstairs, with no underpants, and for the first time since the fifth grade I was overwhelmed with the desire to watch a girl walk upstairs in order to get just a glimpse of what was under her dress. Instead I got the ice and the glasses.

Nellie came down with salami and cheese and brown bread and cherry tomatoes, and I asked her what her pleasure was, and she said "singing." And I said I meant what did she want to drink with her lunch, and she said, "Oh, beer will be fine." And then she helped herself to two shots of bourbon and proceeded to set the table. She produced two damask napkins and two silver napkin rings, and told me she had stolen them from her mother, and that she had lots more upstairs.

"Not the rings, just the napkins. I think I'll have just one more before lunch."

I asked her about the drinking. She said that once when she was little she and a girl friend decided they wanted a drink so they opened a bottle of sherry and drank half and put the half-empty bottle back in the liquor cabinet and that her mother once went to get some sherry because she was kind of a tippler too, and she picked up the bottle and said that the maid must have been at it. Nellie said she knew her mother knew that

16

Tessie—Tessie was the maid—didn't drink and it was obvious that her poor dear mother couldn't remember whether or not she had drunk it herself.

"So after that I could drink all I wanted because my mother couldn't accuse me . . . you know, like honor among thieves?"

I asked her how old she was at the time of the sherry incident and she said, "I think ten going on eleven."

And then she told me with great pride that she had gone to an A.A. meeting—when she first came to New York—and she had met somebody else there who had the exact same history and it depressed her so, that she was just another drunk. So she decided not to reform, and never to go back to A.A. and that if she was going to die she was going to die on her terms and that she absolutely adored drinking and she never got drunk and that, after all, it was the basis of our friendship. That's how we had met. So she'd made the right decision. Right? And we left it at that. It was something neither of us ever brought up again. She saw no point in discussing it, and I didn't want to put myself in the position of policeman. After all, she wasn't my child. She was my gift horse, and whatever she poured down her throat was her own business.

We settled down to our first lunch, silver napkin rings, damask napkins and the smell of garlic and beer and cheese. The salami and cheese were sliced thin but the sandwiches were thick, and Nellie called to my attention the fact that there was butter on the cheese side and mustard on the salami side and no lettuce, and maybe some day if she failed at everything else she could get a job as a sandwichmaker. But then she laughed and said she wasn't going to fail, that she was going to do something somewhere sometime. And she lifted her right arm

17

high in the air and the half of a half of a salami sandwich looked like a beautiful thing, and in an anomalous high, sweet voice that came right out of the twenties she started to sing, and I was embarrassed because I started to cry.

The voice was sweet and moist, and lubricated with lush life, and I was sucked into the center of that sound, that indefinable sound.

> *"Love is*
> *The greatest thing,*
> *The oldest*
> *Yet the latest thing;*
> *I only hope*
> *That Fate will bring*
> *Love's story to you, . . ."*

She created a time warp or gap, whatever they call it, and evoked an era and a *déjà vu* I had felt or heard and seen before. I had known her somewhere else.

> *"Love is*
> *The nicest thing*
> *Old shoes*
> *And ricest thing,*
> *I only hope*
> *That Fate will bring . . ."*

She was totally still and totally in the song and I had to stop crying and smile. Probably half at myself, probably because of the singing.

When she saw that I was smiling she stopped and said, "That was the first Ruth Etting record I ever heard. It was on some weird old disc jockey show real late at night. The guy would take messages from people who were looking for other people or trying to apologize to them or trying to get even with them, and or people

18

who were saying they weren't responsible for bed, board, and bills of other people . . . or people who were begging other people to come home . . . and right in the middle of all those awful messages he played this song, and I had never heard a sound like that. It kind of said everything all the different messages were saying, all the good ones and all the bad ones, and I decided I could sing like that, and I tried and I made the same sound . . . I did . . . and I knew I'd be a singer. Funny? I never could find that station again. I think it came from Baltimore, but you know how radios are."

Her sound was palpable, like the stone in Proust. You step on a stone or a crack and you break your mother's back, and suddenly you're not remembering, you're feeling everything. That's the time gap. Nellie once said that we all were moving and moving, but that time existed in a perfect limbo and never disappeared but just waited for us to come back and possess it again.

And I told her that painting was like that, and she said, "I guess that's what they mean when they talk about having colors in your voice." And we were both very serious and very quiet.

And I fell in love with her.

There we were, she naked under that salmon-pink kimono and me with a rich wife and two children by that wife, and one child by another rich wife, and two children by a poor first and third wife, and one heart attack by myself, and wanting Nellie. And there was Nellie, who was glad that she had met someone in the building that wasn't lousy, and she couldn't have been less interested—with me, that is in love.

That first day she cleaned up the lunch things very quietly, almost pensively, and then she stretched and groaned and asked if she could sleep for a while, and I said that would be fine. She curled up on the sofa and put two pillows under her head, and smiled up at me and asked, "Do you like two pillows or one? I like two. One for your head and one to hold on to." I said that I never slept with a pillow, and she said that was disgusting, and then she dropped right off.

So I started to sketch. I did light ones, funny ones, embryonic-sleeping ones, and when she got up I let her see them, and she asked if she could have one to send home. She said, "I'll tell my mother I've met a young painter. She'll die! Hah! She'd doubly die if she really knew who I'd met. . . . No! Mama would understand that young painters are more doubly dangerous than old painters. Not to cast aspersions on your intentions. . . ?"

She looked through all the sketches and held them to the light, and she looked at them backwards the way some people look at photographs. She said, "God, I do look nubile in them, don't you think?" She looked again and said, "I guess I better tell old Mama that the Art Student's a girl, huh?" And I laughed.

She went home about five and so did I. The first day set the pattern for most of the others.

Nellie was always late and always wanted her beer and always had a treat for lunch. She always greased up with her Elizabeth Arden and always wore the robe like a sarong during the breaks. I think it was her total lack of self or self-consciousness and my overwhelming self-consciousness that made it impossible for me to do or say what I felt about her or for her. Saying or doing anything overt would have violated the trust, the old Painter friendship. It was only when we were totally involved in the painting that I felt I was in control. I was the boss.

And it was only when we discussed painting or *the* painting that she listened with a sense of humility, almost a kind of awe. She would discuss anything else as an equal or an expert—but never painting.

She would sing for me when I asked. Sometimes she'd sing to herself when she was doing lunch or cleaning up, or getting ready to stand. And then I'd stretch my ear to get all the nuances and the colors.

Sometimes I would ask her about her "career" and how it was coming. She'd shrug and say, "You know, sometimes I think I should forget the whole nightclub thing and just go and make a record. Except I don't fit in with the new records, so I have to make a name first. And then when I'm a name, well . . . then the records'll fit in with me."

That sounded almost logical, but I was curious as to how she was going about this business of making a name. She said, "I just go around asking."

I asked her if she had a manager or an agent. She said she couldn't afford one, or maybe one couldn't afford her. So I asked where she went around to do her asking, and she said, "Into the nightclubs, Doperino. I go around five-thirty when the gangsters start to wander in after they've collected the take. It's wild. When I come in they hide the money and pretend they're real people. It's funny, isn't it, when you know someone's faking and they don't know you know?"

I didn't laugh.

"I sing for them . . . it's awful though, because lots of times there's no piano player there yet, so I have to play for myself, and then I can't really do anything with my hands. I guess that's why all those kids sing and play the guitar. With the guitar you can use your hands in some weird kind of dramatic way, and people can get to see that even though you're playing you're using them . . . the hands, I mean, not the people."

Then I laughed, but she didn't laugh with me.

She said, "The guitar just doesn't fit in with what I am. But sooner or later I'll have to break down and learn to

21

use it. Christ, can you just see a guitar with a low-cut black velvet? That's my costume. I didn't tell you?"

She was always vague when she talked about the specifics of what she wanted or what she wanted to do or what she was doing.

Sometimes I used to think that the nightclub story and the Barnard story were big lies, but the whole story pieced together was so crazy that I'd think again and think that it couldn't be anything but the truth. Sometimes I used to think that when she wasn't with me she would just lie on her bed and listen to the television set with the blown-out picture tube, or read her Freshman poetry anthologies, or sing to and for herself.

I suppose I would think those things because I wanted to believe that the essence of her life was totally involved with me and my picture, my painting, my portrait. I knew she had to go out. I knew she had to leave the building, just to breathe. I knew she had to go out to buy food and look for a job. I knew she had to go over to school, just to get those vital report card forms to send to her parents. But then I'd go back to thinking that was a lie too.

I never let myself think about Nellie and other men.

One day she told me she had gotten a job. Down in the Village where she'd been looking. An old Italian had taken her on. She was very excited and said he was old enough to appreciate her style. The next day she told me she had quit the very first night because, "Well, talk about gangsters! I mean, I think he *invented* it!"

She said, "You know, it's disgusting. The gangsters aren't *in* the nightclub business, they *are* the nightclub business. And when they say they like the way you *sing*, well, it's a *double entendre*, if you know what I mean. And no decent girl can have any truck with *that* kind of trash! It's self-destruction. And when you have to choose

22

between self-destruction and the guitar, I guess I'll have to choose the guitar. Because I am basically a nice girl, aren't I? That's from a J. D. Salinger story."

"I know."

"That girl *used* to be a 'nice girl' but I still am one."

"You're very nice."

"Even though I love my body?"

That's where she had me. She was a nice girl who had told an outrageous lie to her parents, had taken money under false pretenses, was posing naked for a lecherous painter, me, and totally convinced that her virtue was inviolable.

She never talked about her parents, she never talked about her friends, except for the male secretary at Barnard who only seemed to function in the forgery department. She seemed to want us to exist in our own vacuum almost as much as I did.

After two or three weeks she offhandedly pronounced that she thought I was good.

I asked her, "As what?" She said, "As a painter."

And then she added, "And as a person. But, *ça va sans dire.*"

It was around then that she began to invite me to dinner. It was all very formal. The invitations were given in advance. I think she had the inherent courtesy—and I use the word "inherent" because it was her word—to know that I'd have to make arrangements with my wife and family about those late nights.

The dinners were the best time and she was an excellent cook. I asked her if her mother had taught her to cook and she said, "Only the boeuf bourguignon. Heavy on the bourguignon. Poor darling. . . ."

The dinners were like the dance of the goony birds. Except there was no mating. . . .

The table was set with a cloth—courtesy of her mother

—the damask napkins, sometimes slightly soiled—candle-light always. Nellie said that was so we could tune out the dirt. The room was small, and the kitchen was a communal kitchen in the hall. There were two Japanese wrestling teachers, old ones, she said, who lived down the hall and kept seaweed and raw fish in the icebox. "Can you imagine? Here I am with a communal kitchen and nothing worth stealing in the fridge, either for them or me!"

She had one of those Indian-print bedspreads and a standing lamp and a table for a desk and some books and a huge drawing of Oscar Wilde. She said she really didn't like Dirty Oscar, but it was the biggest, cheapest drawing she could find. She had some old sheet music covers of Ruth Etting and Helen Morgan pasted up with Scotch tape.

No vestiges of her own life, no feeling of her own past or future.

She had a Victrola. She had picked it up at the Salvation Army. And some old records. She never played Morgan or Etting—comparisons are odiferous she said—but sometimes she played Russ Columbo and sometimes Jack Buchanan. She adored Russ Columbo. She'd play "I Called To Say Goodnight" over and over. Sometimes we'd dance to Russ Columbo, sometimes we'd dance to Nellie—to her voice.

I was always terrified that I'd have an attack in her apartment. I would take her in my arms and tremble, and either she didn't notice—and I can't believe that—or she chose to ignore the trembling, and I can believe that. I began to look forward to the dinners as much as the daytimes. I used to tell my wife that at last I was doing something important and that I wanted to work late, and she would say, "Bloody charming—a good one—coming from someone that doesn't have to work at all."

• • •

Our dinners were fun and they were funny. Part of having a good time. Nellie made it seem like one of those phoney, very chic 1930s movies. She would put on a Katharine Hepburn act up-dated with a dash of Audrey Hepburn. We never drank bourbon before dinner. Always martinis, straight up, and hors d'oeuvres and something you could cook in one pot . . . that was so she didn't have to make trips between the room and the communal kitchen, and *salade,* always *salade.* She said the crunchiness of the *salade* set off the softness of stroganoff or the curry or the stuffed cabbage.

She would imitate Zsa Zsa Gabor when she did the cabbage. Once she made the bourguignon and it was delicious and she looked up at me and said, "The old bitch *really* knew some things, didn't she? My mother."

Except for things like that she rarely talked about her parents. She began not to offer any information about whether or not they still believed she was in school or whether or not they sent her any money or whether or not they were rich or poor. I never even knew where she came from. Sometimes she would drop funny things like, "My mother never let me go out of the house without clean underwear because you never knew whether or not you'd be run over and wouldn't it be terrible if the people at the hospital saw you with rotten-looking underwear? But Christ, if I were run over and killed it wouldn't matter to me because I'd be dead. It would just be a disgrace for her—my mother."

And if I had had the style to play the Clark Gable in her movie I would have leaned over the table and said, "It would matter to me." But I didn't. Because I was boxed in by Nellie and her rules. She had set them down without advice or consent, and I abided by them because I had no choice, and so I never said that if she were run

25

over and killed it would matter to me more than anything in the world.

One night at dinner she got up from the table and lifted the bedspread and showed me a suitcase. She said, "It's all packed!"

She said she always kept that packed suitcase under the bed because you never knew when you had to get out of town. She said that her mother had taught her to do that; that her mother always kept a packed suitcase under the bed because she never knew when she couldn't take her father any more.

Now, if I had been a normal person, or better yet, if she had been a normal person, I would have said very casually, "I'd like to know a little more about your mother and your father and what they're like and where you come from." Any normal person, given that opening, would have asked those questions of another normal person. But instead I said, "You want a drink?"

"Hmm-mmmm."

Affirmative.

We had a drink and she said, "When they make potboilers do they mix the whiskey with the beer?"

"No, they drink it as a chaser."

"The whiskey or the beer?"

"Very funny."

"I'm not being funny. I'm curious."

"The beer's the chaser."

"Let's split one."

So there went the opportunity to find out about the parents. And Nellie would have told me that it was probably because I really didn't want to find out. And she probably would have been right. Secrets were part of the rules, part of the image . . . the crazy quilt, ragbag image, the wandering princess in disguise who sang a song for a shot of bourbon. Circe with a salami sandwich. And

I loved it. I loved the shades and shadows and echos that could be interpreted through the multiple choice system. I was willing to play the game and seal the vacuum and have the Nellie that existed only in a salmon-pink limbo. And I understood why it was, "Ask me no questions so I don't have to tell you any lies." We both knew without saying that if the answers were wrong the image would dissolve, would disappear, and there would be no Nellie and no painting, no picture, no portrait. And I knew that you couldn't photograph a ghost but that you could give life to a figment of your imagination.

So Nellie didn't hold a modest hand over one breast, and her hair wasn't quite long enough to serve as a fig leaf, and I wasn't Botticelli, and she wasn't Venus. But I knew there was water somewhere and that I held the divining rod. Nellie said we would find a Pleasure Dome and the Fountain of Youth and Saratoga Springs all rolled into one. One day she walked in and said, "You're mine best friend." She was in her Semitic period. So I said, "That's good." And she said, "I only told you so you shouldn't worry."

It must have been five or six weeks before I realized that what I thought had been good work was really surface stuff, brush work. It must have taken that long and that many songs and dinners and jokes and gangster stories for me to begin to move inside that painting.

But one day, there I was, inside. And what had been free and easy and exhilarating and fun to do became passionate and possessive and overwhelming and exhausting. And I worked with such a fury that my hand shook. It was a love affair with me and that painting. And I wasn't making love to it, but with it. Every day I'd go deeper and deeper inside, and of course Nellie knew. She never said she knew. She expected her rules to be kept by herself as well as others, but I knew that she knew that the work was different. She stood just as still as ever but —there was one thing—she'd hum or sing to herself. She knew that I was with the painting and not with her . . . except, of course, during the breaks.

Once she did say, "You don't mind me singing while you work now?" And I told her no, and she said, "You don't really hear me though, do you? Or if you do hear a sound it's the painting, and not me. But I don't care because it's all the same. And it's good practice . . . for me, I mean."

So she'd sing and the sound—the sound and the way she held her head—became the essence of the picture. And I was working, really working. And I was exultant, delirious, and good to everyone, and good to myself, and my wife made the pronouncement that we had come through a bad period and that now maybe things would eventually work out. And that was fine because she laid off me.

One day after lunch, Nellie lay down on the sofa with her two pillows but she didn't go to sleep. She lay there watching me. I couldn't keep away from the picture. There was something in the hands that was wrong. She had a crooked thumb, the real Nellie—and I wanted it to be right in the painting, and I knew it was wrong. And I didn't need her to pose. I could fix it without her. So I started to work and then I heard her move, and I glanced over at her and saw that her eyes were all the way open. And that her mouth was open, and I saw that look of orgiastically innocent lust on her face, and I saw that she was trembling. So I put down the brush and walked over and pulled away the salmon-pink kimono, and we made love.

It was lousy. She was half drunk, and I was so excited that I could barely begin, much less finish, and I knew that where I was spent and sated and ashamed, she was writing in the agony of being neither here nor there, and she put her robe around her and got up and said, "I want to go home. I'll see you tomorrow." And I said, "I'm sorry," and she said, "There's nothing to be sorry for. I wanted it too." And I said, "Will I see you tomorrow?" and she said, "Sure. I just said so, didn't I?" and she ran upstairs.

I didn't see her for eight days. I listened for her footsteps, I pounded on the ceiling with my broom. I walked upstairs and pounded on the door. I peered under her doorsill looking for a light. I left notes of apology, then notes of defiance and explanation, and pushed them under her door. I put things on the basis that she had failed me professionally. I promised never to do anything like that again. Once I even wrote a note about my heart and used that as an excuse for my failure. That one I didn't push under the door. I grew to loathe the painting and myself. My wife and children seemed like heartless animals, and I treated them as such. But I couldn't stay away from the studio and the painting.

One morning I pounded on the ceiling until I thought the plaster would come down. Then I stopped, and I think I began to sweat and shiver out of sheer rage and frustration and disgust with myself. But there were footsteps upstairs and miracle of miracles, I heard her door open and close, and I turned my back on my own door, and then I heard my own door open and close, and she said, "Hi. I'm late." She slipped off her robe and "assumed her stance" and I picked up my brush and started mixing the colors.

With the lunch hour came the ritual. She made sandwiches and we sat to eat, and I asked her where she'd been.

"Nowhere special."

"Did you go home?"

"Home to where?"

"Home to your family?"

"No."

So I asked her who she'd been seeing. And she told me, "No one that you would know. Want half of my half, I'm full." And she handed me half of her half of a sandwich and there it was, the rules. Just as if nothing had happened to change them. But then she said, "Did you miss me?" And I told her "yes," and she said, "I missed you too, a lot."

She wanted everything to be exactly as it had been. She wasn't pretending, either. And if I wanted anything from her I had to play along. So I played, but I was pretending.

I began to suspect her of everything. The kind of suspicion you have for someone that has no obligation to you is the worst kind. You lose the joy in what they give you because you're so intent on finding if they're giving the same thing to someone else.

I began turning down her dinner invitations, and of course, she acted as if it didn't faze her one way or the other. Once she said to me, "I guess things are getting better for you at home, and that's good because after you're a three-time loser, and you get convicted, the fourth time it's mandatory life. You know what I mean? —Unless the judge is nice. And when you've been divorced three times you just know that you're in bad for life. I'd never marry anybody that was married three times. I mean, I'm bad enough without taking on extra problems. But you're not a problem. You're good for me. People just looking at us and our situation and everything would think we were bad for each other. But we're not. I mean, with working together and the painting and our schedule, it's kind of like a built-in Children's Hour,

30

huh? For all I know, I'll be the one to save your marriage. Wouldn't that be wild?"

"I told you not to talk while I'm working."

"I'll sing."

"Sing."

She sang,

"I used to dream
That I would discover
The perfect lover
Some day——"

I don't know if she knew she was telling me off, but oh, God, was she telling me! I put the brush down and I looked at her. And then she said, "Why'd you stop working?"

I told her I didn't feel like working.

Nellie said, "Look. If I were you—and I am—I would stop staring at me and do some work. I mean, you make me feel like a freak at a peep show. So you better hurry! Hurry! Hurry! You've got a lot to do before you're finished."

She said the last like a carney barker.

I said, "How do you know what I've done and what I've got to do. You've never looked at the picture."

"I don't have to."

"Why?"

"I don't know."

"Why?"

"Why don't I know, or why don't I look?"

"Why don't you look?"

"Because it's like looking at somebody who hasn't yet put their false teeth in. It's not fair."

"To me?"

31

"To both of us. I mean, I've been holding my end up. . . ." She laughed. "Boy, have I. I'd like to see you stand like me. Let me tell you, it's not easy. But come on, come out. Move! Move! Don't pretend you've turned to stone. I may be a lot of people, but I'm not Medusa."

She used to stand—I used to make her stand—for hours. Totally still, totally silent. And then I would stare. At Nellie, not at the painting. I would glance at the girl in the painting, but I would stare at the real one. The girl in the painting had been done by another man, maybe it was even a picture of another girl done by another man. And, I couldn't go inside that painting any more. Nellie knew it, and it hurt her because she had believed in the project outlined for mutual immortality and she could see it floundering.

She shamed me into beginning again, very slowly, almost defiantly. I felt like a nineteenth-century German caught between young Werther and the Prussian High Command. Which was which? Who was who? I don't know. But there was something vaguely Germanic in the way I went at the work. *Eins,* zwei, drei . . . *eins,* zwei, drei.

Like a child doing scales at the piano.

No good.

Faking, just exercising.

Nellie knew it. One day she walked in and didn't take off the robe but leveled her eyes and said, "Listen! You pretend you're Frank Sinatra and that I'm Ava Gardner and that we're inevitable . . . that's what the painting should be. Okay?"

Eins, zwei, drei, *eins,* zwei, drei. . . .

It wasn't Nellie's fault. She was pushing me uphill with her nose. She was trying desperately to defy inertia, trying to create a new momentum, trying to pull me out of the loser's gully. Whose bootstraps she was using is a moot point. Needless to say, the Sinatra-Gardner image didn't work.

Eins, zwei, drei . . .

When spring came she couldn't decide whether or not to get a huge pair of sunglasses. She said, "I just don't *know*. I mean, you see them all over on everybody so they're out, and that's awful, but they're nice. And I get stinging eyes from the sun so it's fair for me to wear them. The real kind, the kind I want, are forty-three dollars, but they sell ones for three dollars that look pretty much like the forty-three-dollar ones, and that makes the forty-three's a waste. . . . So! I've decided to stay out of the sun during the day, and wear the three-dollar kind indoors and drink nothing but champagne!"

"You're going to drink nothing but champagne?"

"*We* are. I want *you* to stock it for me. It won't be very expensive. You can buy the New York State kind and wrap it in one of my napkins and I'll never know it's not the real thing."

I told her that it wasn't considered good form to ask someone to stock champagne for you and she was terribly hurt. She said, "Well, I've never asked you for anything else, have I? And painters are supposed to do things like that. You should have *suggested* it. Long ago. Not me. . . ." She looked embarrassed for a moment and then she said, "I like it on the rocks! Disgusting, but I do."

I stocked the champagne and we both drank it on the rocks and ate egg salad with olives and dill on thin slices of pumpernickel bread. Once Nellie scooped out the last of the egg salad and smeared it on the last piece of bread and handed it to me with, "That's your dividend for not coming to dinner any more."

"Do you want me to?"

"It's polite to wait till you're asked."

33

"I've been asked."

"Not lately."

"Eating all alone?"

"No—I eat with the Japs. It's very economical. When I invite them they can't stand my food, and when they invite me, I can't stand theirs, so we all save money." She took another drink and started to laugh in the bubbles. "Of course, I'm not eating with the Japs. Christ, you know how I feel about *them*. . . . I mean, not just *them*, I mean all Japs."

"That's stupid."

"It is not. It's a moral position. They *sneaked*. . . ."

"And when we sneak?"

"First of all, we don't sneak, and second of all when we *do*—well, that's commando warfare. . . . Don't you read?"

"I was *there*."

"*There?*"

"No—but I was alive."

"Then I probably have a much better point of view than you." She picked up the bottle and held it to the light and drained the dregs and read the label and set it down, and said, "Let's put candles in every one we drink and see how many we finish and when we've got a lot let's open a shooting gallery."

"Are you drunk?"

"Never."

"You want a nap?"

"No. I'm floating. For real. Let's work. Do me with bubbles, or maybe inside a bubble. Let's really work."

"I'm too old to run in your horse race, Nellie."

"I'm not running one."

"I am."

"Well, don't. When I said you were my best friend, I really meant it. Please. . . ."

"I can't."

"Try—try it Yogi."

"I have been."

"Then try something else, but try. Because if you don't do it I'll *die* and you'll never have any of me, and if you *do*, you'll have me forever."

She went out of my life in the same way that she had come into it. She left in her way, quite suddenly, with no warnings. But this time she had the grace to make a pronouncement. She broke the Children's Hour pattern and knocked at my door at nine or ten in the evening. She said she had seen a light under the doorsill and was delighted that I hadn't gone home yet. She told me that she had found a job, a real job, and I told her that I had heard that before. And she said that this wasn't like before, it was different, it was kosher. She was moving to Boston, and wasn't it terrific that she had part of her clothes packed. You know, the clothes in the suitcase under the bed. It seemed that she had a job singing in a nightclub in Boston.

She said, "Boston's a very big music town."

Boston was a big music town, and I started to sweat.

"I've made a great contact with a man who is *definitely* not a gangster."

When I asked her how she knew he definitely wasn't a gangster she explained that she could smell it, and then she said, "I mean literally not figuratively. Most of them, most gangsters either smell B.O. or hair tonic or bad cologne and this man doesn't smell like any of those."

She said the job was going to be in a very hightoned club where they don't let the people eat and clank when the performers are performing, and that the man was going to let her wear her low-cut black velvet dress and give her an accompanist so she could sit on the piano, which would be lovely because she could really use her

35

hands and really do her Helen Morgan, and then she added quite casually that she was leaving in two weeks so I'd better finish the painting. And there it was down and dirty. Put up or shut up. Do me or don't. Love me or leave me. Or both.

And finally I began to work. Not quite the way I had at one time. Not quite consumed, not quite inside. I could never be there any more and that hadn't been painting, anyway. It had been hypnotism and mesmerism. The painting had been the Ouija board and I the medium. Now I was again the painter, in control and determined to finish. After all, I didn't want Nellie to die. I wanted to have her always, and if this was the only way, then I would take what I could get. Nellie used to say, "You gets what you like if you like what you gets."

I let her talk to me while I worked. And I listened or I didn't listen while she rattled on about her career and how she would be discovered in Boston, and how she finally really understood about the suitcase under the bed, because it didn't mean running away any more . . . it meant getting a chance to go someplace.

I didn't ask her what arrangements she had made about school or whether or not she had told her parents she was going to Boston. I didn't ask her if she had a place to live or where I could get in touch with her. I, too, had rules.

We began to have dinner together again. We were both tired, because the days were long, so the dinners were quiet and sleepy, and sometimes she'd do "her act" for me. I liked it. I would applaud after every number and call *bis, bis* and she would laugh and pour me another drink.

When I went home I would try to talk to my wife. I would try to prepare for a life that could be predicated on existence without salami and cheese and champagne

36

on the rocks, without Elizabeth Arden and Helen Morgan and Russ Columbo. My wife said that I'd been working so much and so hard that I ought to be ready for a show, and I told her maybe. And I laughed to myself, because I knew that show or no show I would never show the painting of Nellie. Especially to my wife.

I finished. The two weeks were over and Nellie was packed. She had the small bag, the one she kept under the bed, and she had a trunk which was being shipped to Boston. She told me I could have Oscar Wilde and the bedspread and anything else I wanted. She gave me a bottle of Cordon Rouge 880 and she said, "It's brut, but *ça va sans dire*. The man at the liquor store said it was the best, and he sold it to me. I guess I look over eighteen now."

I opened the champagne and Nellie said, "Now can I see the painting?"

It was covered with a sheet.

I started to take the sheet away, as Nellie closed her eyes and screwed them tight and hunched up her whole body as if she were Martha Graham preparing to meet her maker.

I guess she was.

She said, "Now?"

I said, "Now."

She opened her eyes and looked. There was no sound from her. And then she began to cry.

She said, "She has no face. Why doesn't she have a face?"

I couldn't explain. So I just told her that I was a painter.

And she said, "I paint what I see, said Rivera to John D.'s grandson Nelson?"

She asked me if I knew the poem and I said I did and she said, "You know everything that I know."

I told her I wished I did.

The Writer

I was the writer in Nellie's life, and therefore it is incumbent upon me to write a epitaph for her. Not one to be engraved upon a tombstone. Just an epitaph for someone who deserved one, and would have liked to have had one. Nellie would have said, "Doesn't everybody?" And I would have said, "Get one or want one, it depends."

She would have asked, "Depends on what?" I would have answered, "On how they died." Then she would have said, "Better yet, on how they lived . . . but ugggh, that sounds like Norman Vincent Peale!"

Nellie lived on the edge of her own personal precipice with a built-in banana peel to match, and she died right on schedule.

She always said she'd never get past twenty-two. She used to say, "I'll make twenty-one because I'll get all my rights. But twenty-two is another story. Twenty-two is down and dirty and no more free and easy. Twenty-two is really going on forty, and I won't fit. I'm like Alice."

"Alice who?"

> *"Alice, where art thou going?*
> *Upstairs to take a bath*
> *Alice with legs like toothpicks*
> *And a neck like a giraffe*
> *Alice, where art thou going?*
> *Glub, Glub, Glub. . . ."*

Nellie didn't have legs like toothpicks and her neck—while long—was nowhere near a giraffe's. Legs and neck withstanding, she always called her shots right, and twenty-two was the house number. *"Faites vos jeux. Rien ne va plus."*

I was in Rome when I learned that she had killed herself. Mike Isaacs cabled me in words of one syllable that said, "Your fault." It wasn't my fault . . . it wasn't anybody's fault.

We were all to blame.

Even Nellie. First, last and foremost—Nellie.

Nevertheless, as I said, I'm the writer, and here goes the epitaph.

In case you're interested, my credits and qualifications include short stories, novels, plays, some light political analyses, a few soft advertisements, a goodly number of television plays—both Eastern and Western—a screen play or two, some good and bad letters, the same for checks, laundry lists, application blanks, status reports, and ungodly requests of the Veterans Administration. I am now proceeding to add epitaphs to my repertoire. It may be the making of me.

I could begin my epitaph for Nellie by saying,

> *"I sing of Nellie strong and proud*
> *Whose warmest heart recoiled at war. . . ."*

That's stolen from e. e. cummings, and is pertinent and applicable, but stolen.

So I might say,

> *"She walks in beauty like the night*
> *Of cloudless climes and starry skies. . . ."*

Lord Byron, who was one of Nellie's favorites. It's very fitting and quite beautiful, but it belongs to Lord Byron and I must try to make this my own, for Nellie.

I could say,

> *"A sweet disorder in the dress*
> *Kindled a willful wantonness. . . ."*

That's an emendation from Robert Herrick. Nellie was very big on emendations.

I should begin by saying:

> *"Forgive me, Nellie,*
> *For I know not what I did."*

I met her in Boston where we had both gone on wild goose chases, she in search of a star, and me in search of a stomach lining. Neither can be found anywhere, much less in Boston. If I sound bitter it's because I am and was. I was very bitter then.

A wife, of course, was the problem. A wife who was not a wife, but very much a wife; a wife who was totally mine, and not at all or ever mine; a wife whom I needed desperately not to have. A wife.

When I didn't have her I married her, when I married

her I didn't want her, when she left me, I didn't have her so I had to get her back; and when I got her back I wanted someone else's wife; and then my wife and the someone else's wife both found me out and left me, and neither of this was good for my work nor my stomach, and what had been a fashionable ulcer became an agonizing belly. Therefore Boston.

Boston is a Mecca for all the sick people in the world. They flock to Boston to find out about their outsides and insides and ulcers and hernias and kidneys and gallstones, and especially their blood and their livers. Boston's very big on blood and livers. It's common knowledge that when a doctor disagrees as to what is right or wrong with a paying patient he looks over his shoulder or at his colleague, lights a cigarette, turns to the patient and says, "Why don't you go up to the Peter Bent Brigham in Boston? They'll really work you up, up there!" This is a sure sign that the doctor doesn't know what's wrong with you and is too busy to operate. In my case the doctor didn't know what to do with or for me and didn't feel the urge to operate. He was baffled by an ulcer that didn't behave like other ulcers.

I could have told him that I was not suffering from a bleeding ulcer, but much more significantly, a bad image. Therefore, the quirks.

I was delighted with the idea of going out of town. It put my stomach beyond the pale of the greatest city in the world, it gave me a sense of crossing the bar to the greatest unknown. Galahad in search of Gelusil. Women would weep. Not phone, weep. And letters were my milieu.

And there was a very convenient sister in Boston. My sister. I would be gone, but not really out from under the proverbial familial roof. I would be seeking refuge within my wife's mixed-up idea of the Hopi-Zuni structure. Very tribal, it seemed. I would be trying to make that marriage work but not having to make the effort. A very good system for rekindling the image of the husband who never leaves the hearth, even in distress. And I look very good from afar.

As I left I wondered if the other lady in question, the someone else's wife, might not even be impressed enough to be rekindled a little. She was sure to hear everything from my wife. They were friends. Best friends.

My sister was delighted by the prospect of my journey North. With me in Boston she wouldn't have to get her blow-by-blows long distance.

I applied and was accepted and allowed to enter the hospital. Getting into the Peter Bent Brigham is a bit like getting into Harvard. They worked me up and down and thank God, I was out of town because, talk about images, I was Mr. Bellyache. And if there was anything they could have removed, I would have parted with it with pleasure. If I felt lousy when I went in, I felt worse as time went on. They say that many of the great medical techniques our doctors are using today were developed in the laboratories of Nazi Germany. I believe it.

I also believe that they go out of their way to surround you with despair and disgust. You reach a point where you believe the other patients come, not from the real world outside, but from Central Casting. My play was No Exit. I had three roommates, all incurable, all moribund, all tiptoeing through the tulips on the great divide.

My first roommate, Mr. Veinleif, cried all the time. It was a malady. He was a railroad lineman and he had been worried about being automated. One day he started to cry and just never stopped. He liked the hospital and he was getting all his RR Brotherhood benefits, but he wept.

42

The Chief Resident would come in and say, "How do you feel today, Mr. Veinleif?" and Mr. Veinleif would blubber, "I feel much better than yesterday, doctor." There was something wrong with his tear ducts, but he didn't have to go to Boston to figure that out.

There he was, opposite me, dripping away . . . the worst was when he cried himself to sleep.

In the bed next to Mr. Veinleif was Teenchy Moroni. He liked being called Teench for short. His real name was George.

I called him George.

Teenchy was not an epithet for George, it was a euphemism.

He was in Boston for the fat operation.

He explained that even though they did it in New York they did it better in Boston. The fat operation consists of digging beneath the epidermis and extracting large amounts of fat. It is performed when the considered opinion of the doctors is that the patient would take more than a lifetime to lose the weight in question.

Teenchy George had an operation every eight or ten days. They were always performed upon one specific area of his body, so he was always lopsided. Some days he'd be thin on top and fat on the bottom, some days thin on the left and fat on the right. Some days thin in front, fat behind. You should have seen him the day they did the first half of the behind!

He read pornographic comic books and got angry if I asked him when and if he had ever seen his so-called genitalia. I think he hadn't been laid in so long that his memory of sex and the female body was glorious beyond any semblance of the real thing. He couldn't wait to be sliced down to what he called "a fighting chance."

My third roommate was an undertaker. He had the

everlasting stench of formaldehyde and a diaphragmatic hernia that had been botched at Johns Hopkins. Talk about coals to Newcastle. He lived in Boston.

He had a wife, and she was running the Funeral Parlor while Mr. Fischer was incapacitated. She had become adept at the art of embalming and had that inescapable odor—matching his—to prove it. But being a woman, she tried to camouflage hers. God knows where she found her cologne. I once asked her if she knew that Eskimo women bathed themselves in urine and she said she didn't see what that had to do with anything.

We who have been educated in the wasteful and winsome ways of the Modern American Funeral think we know everything.

Think not thou art wise.

I, who now have a Ph.D. in Funerals—courtesy of Mrs. Fischer—have developed a healthy respect for death. When I go, I pray that there are no remains. The defective airplane, the acid bath tub—fine with me. Just no remains.

Since I had the honor of being placed beside the venerable and kindly Mr. Fischer I was privileged to listen to a full description of every day's activities. Mrs. Fischer felt that I listened with interest and respect, and every so often she would look over at me and smile as if to say, "We'll give you one hell of a sendoff!"

After ten days of Veinleif's tears and George's lopsided ass, and Mr. Fischer's "You're all heart and class," I made a most reasonable request to be transferred to the psychiatric ward, but the request was denied.

Instead I was granted a parole—in custody of my sister.

The doctors felt I had had my share of barium milkshakes and had given my due of urine and blood. They realized that it would be impossible to X-ray, measure, stick, or contort my feeble body any more, and that before sending me to the Smithsonian they would "analyze and interpret" me. They assured me that I would get my answers in a few weeks. At that time I believed it would take a few weeks because Boston is so brilliantly thorough. Later I found out it was because their key stomach man was in Greece.

They asked for my sister's address, in case they needed me, and I didn't want to give it to them because I knew that if I died before the analyses were done I could be shipped right over to the Fischers' and everybody would cry—over my dead body. But, having been in the army, I obeyed the commands of the Red Tape Brigade. I paid, signed out, genuflected in the direction of the bursar and told them not to send a copy of anything to my wife.

Thereupon I bade fond farewell to life in the lunatic corner and moved body and soul to Cambridge and the lunatic fringe. My sister worked part-time in a clinic for pre-school-age schizophrenics, and my brother-in-law sat at M.I.T. thinking up a machine that would reproduce itself. As far as I'm concerned one's job was predicated on the other's, and their child was a combination of both. They lived the life of all graduate students who go to school in Boston and can never leave. They prolong their Ph.D.'s with an incestuous passion. It's as if once their theses were accepted they would have to face Dr. Strangelove. Nevertheless, it was middle-class luxury on the Charles, and pastrami at Wursthaus, and Culture, culture everywhere and not a drop to drink. The ulcer had made liquor *verboten*. The agenda was lousy with organ music and Marianne Moore, and the Fogg. But every writer must have his Boston period.

I had no work to do but my own.

And I couldn't work.

I was waiting for a picture deal to come through from Hollywood. I thought about doing a piece on Veinleif, or maybe on Veinleif and George and Fischer. The interaction and my dispassionate eye would have been very *New Yorker*. Then I realized I would make more money doing a doctor show for television. Three pathetic characters, and me. I would have made myself a criminal. . . . I called my agent. No word on the screen play, but high hopes. Television show? *New Yorker?* Save it. . . . A major insight.

I got sympathy from my sister, a jaundiced eye from my brother-in-law, no letters from my wife. She was getting her blow-by-blows from Cambridge. Obviously my wife and my sister had decided that the inscrutable, unattainable image would be most effective. For what?

I was getting very little of anything, and then I remembered about Nellie.

Mike Isaacs had told me that there was a girl I should definitely look up if and when I went to Boston. He said she was a rejuvenation if you were getting old, and a slap in the face if you were getting smug, and a good-time Charlie if you wanted to have a good time. He said she was a "golden girl" for fake and for real.

I had many reservations about such a rave review. I knew Mike Isaacs' wife all too well to trust his judgment. But he had never called his wife a good-time Charlie, much less a good time, and I needed both so I went looking for Nellie.

At this point Nellie would say, "Christ—here you are writing my epitaph and you've just gotten around to me. . . ." And then she would have opened her mouth and eyes and inhaled a lot of air and said, "So! It was Mike's wife that was the someone else's wife. . . . You're disgusting!"

"Dear Nell
Ding Dong Bell
Ding Dong Diddle
The farmer's in the dell.
Dear Nell
Don't tell
They'll hang you from a Wishing Well
And when the Wishing Well goes dry
They'll bake you in a pie in the sky
And when the pie in the sky falls flat
They'll sell you for a hatpin . . .
Much less a hat."

The aforesaid is not part of my epitaph for Nellie. It's part of my remembrance. She once recited the poem to me. It had been written for her by a young actor, a very young actor, she had known in New York. She had met him when she saw him do an off-Broadway reading of a James Joyce hodgepodge.

She said the poem was a little dirty and vaguely derivative, but it pleased her that someone had thought enough of her to write a poem about her, even though he wasn't a poet.

I agreed. He was not a poet. Actors are actors, not poets, and the poem was not a poem. Maybe it was the story of Nellie's life.

But back to my epitaph.

"Oh, Nellie, I'm heartily sorry for having
       offended you,
And I detest all my sins
Because I dread the loss of heaven, and the
       pains of hell.
But most of all, I am sorry for having offended you
Who art all good and worthy of my love."

I save all the letters I get and make carbons of all the ones I write for the academician whose duty it will be to analyze my life in relation to my collected works—so I dug out a postcard from Mike asking if I'd gone to see Nellie yet and I got the name of the club that she was working at. I borrowed my sister's car. The car was mistake number one. Boylston Street is no place to park. I took two Gelusil, put the car in a parking lot, walked into the club and sat down at a table. Mistake number two. It cost me five dollars. Then I ordered a drink. Mistake number three.

There had been no mention of a Nellie outside on the marquee or inside on the billboards, and no semblance of anything resembling Nellie at or near the bandstand, and I inquired of the general factotum as to when and where she appeared. Sleazily—if that's not correct, it's descriptive—he told me that she was no longer with them, but that he knew where I could find her.

The Tattletale Club was on Hollis Street behind the old Metropolitan Theatre. It should have been called One Step Beyond.

But they had a parking lot. I went in and asked the hatcheck girl if I could see the singer, and the hatcheck girl said, "What singer?" and I told her. The hatcheck girl asked why I wanted to see her and I explained that a friend suggested I call upon her, and the hatcheck girl asked who the friend was. I thought she was going to take a message to Nellie's dressing room, so I said a Mr. Isaacs from New York and the hatcheck girl looked me over and she said, "I'm her."

Of course she had to be her.

I would never have called her golden. I would have said closer to burnished, but that's the difference between an adjective and an adverb.

48

"Her" is a pronoun and was still a question mark.

Nellie said, "Sit down and I'll get you a glass of milk."

I looked, and she laughed and explained that she knew I must be the man with the ulcer, and I asked her how she knew. She said that Mike had sent her a postcard a few weeks before saying he was sending her a present with an ulcer. She said, "I'll tell you what, I'll make you a milk punch. It's part milk and part brandy with rum and cinnamon and nutmeg." And I must have looked sick because she said, "I'll split it with you. You know, like Lucrezia Borgia."

We finally settled on brandy. I asked her when she got off and she said anytime she wanted, 'cause it was late enough—that no more people would come in and anyone who had anything worthwhile checking had already checked out. So I asked her why she stayed and she said, "Kind of like obligation. You know, they've been very nice to me." And then she told me the story of how she hadn't been a big hit in Boston.

It seems that Helen Morgan in a black velvet dress on the piano hadn't evoked an era. Instead, it had evoked a lot of talking and a lot of walking out and eventually a lot of empty tables, and the nice man who ran the Boylston Street club turned out to be not so nice when it came to empty tables, but the nice man who ran the Tattletale Club understood her problems and "dug" her talent and let her go to work as the hatcheck girl with a little singing thrown in on the side.

"I don't feel bad about it because Boylston Street leads to trouble and the band here is very protective and very encouraging." The band consisted of five men in their late forties or early fifties who looked like unsuccessful cloak-and-suiters. It later turned out they were.

"The band plays outside dates. You know, weddings

and parties and Bar Mitzvahs and Elks and even the American Legion, and once in a while the cripple wards. Boston is lousy with cripples."

I told her I knew.

"And when they play these dates they take me along, and I can sing. They're all old—in the band, not the audience—and they like the way I sing, and it's good practice and good money, so it's not a total loss. You're sure you don't want milk? Or even water? It would cancel out the brandy. That's how Helen Morgan could drink all the time. She would take one milk and one brandy, or one water and one brandy, and she said they canceled each other out. Someone who really knew her told me that for real."

I said, "But she drank herself to death," and she said, "But she never knew she was doing it." I said, "But she died," and Nellie said, "Doesn't everybody?"

My dear, dead Logician.

I asked her if we could go now and she said, "Where?" and I told her I wanted to get out of the Club. And she said, "I do, too. I mean, for good. I've got to get out of here sooner or later."

I assured her I was interested only in both of us leaving that particular place at that particular time and she said, "Some present you are. Mike said you were a mud runner."

"I don't get it."

"I don't have time to explain, but it has to do with horse races."

She said goodbye to someone in the kitchen and she waved goodbye to everyone in the band, and we walked out of the Club onto the street and she started toward the Kenmore Square subway stop, and I told her I had a car. That delighted her. She said, "If you have a car you can take me to Nantasket." She said, "I don't mean now, I mean some Sunday. Saul, he's in the band, has a house in Nantasket on the beach and I love it because it's just like Long Beach. Have you ever been there? I mean, to Long Beach." I said I had. She said, "Nantasket is just as Jewish as Long Beach and right in the middle of all the fried clams they have lox and bagels and it reminds me of New York. It's a terrific beach, I mean Nantasket, not Long Beach, and there's hardly anybody there except for the kids.

"Will you take me to the beach?"

I said, "Sure."

We walked to the car and she said, "I guess it too late to go anywhere so you'd better take me home. I live in Cambridge. That's so when I write to my parents they think I'm going to Radcliffe. I'll show you the way. We go all the way up Commonwealth Avenue but we don't take Storrow Drive because I hate expressways. I like to look at the houses on Commonwealth—so we go up Commonwealth and we take the Cottage Farm Bridge which is my favorite. . . ."

I let her know that I, too, resided in Cambridge and knew the way to carry the sleigh and requested her address and telephone number for the addenda.

Somehow, somewhere, someone had given Nellie a sense of herself that had made her believe she had a capacity and capability to touch, feel, and express the essence of Life itself. She believed that she was golden.

I think Mike Isaacs must have been the one who convinced her. She spoke of him all the way home, all the way along the Charles. She spoke with great affection and a supposedly matronly understanding. It made me sad, sad for him. Nellie never understood that he was in love with her. And he never knew with whom he was in love. Painters are people who create their own images,

51

and as God created Eve from Adam, he created Nellie.

I thought Nellie was amusing, but not really much more. At that time.

We arrived at her house. I asked if I might come up and she vamped and said, "To see me sometime?" She thought that was very, very funny and laughed too loud, and then she put her hand over her mouth and shut herself up, and she was in one instance the chastised child and the chastiser.

She had a bedroom and half a kitchen and half a bathroom in somebody's house in Cambridge. It had obviously been the servants' quarters. She told me the people who owned the house were deaf, and wasn't that a blessing? For her, not them.

High on a shelf, in her clothes closet, were brandy and bourbon and we started on the bourbon. She raised her glass and asked me what I did, and I told her I was a writer. She said, "Cheers." And she asked me what I wrote. I said I wrote short stories. She said, "What kind of short stories?" I said, "All kinds." She said, "Murders?" I said, "Yes." She said, "No love stories?" I said, "A few." She said, "Aren't you always scared that the people you're writing about will know it's them?" And I explained that was the chance you took.

She said, "What was the first story you ever wrote?" And I told her that the first story I ever wrote was about a boy who asked a girl to a dance. She asked me if the story had been published. I said, "Yes."

"The first story you ever wrote was published?"

"It was."

"Did the girl recognize herself?"

I told her she wasn't a real girl and she said, "I bet she was." I said, "Well, I never saw her again so it didn't matter." And she said, "That's rotten."

She asked where I came from and what I was doing in

Boston. She asked me if I was married and when I told her yes, she said, *"C'est entendu*—which is slang for 'my luck.'"

We both knew the translation, if not accurate, was indeed apropos.

She asked me about my ulcer and I told her about the hospital and my roommates, and she said I was heartless and that she used to think writers were, or were supposed to be, the souls of understanding, but that in the last analysis—that always fascinated me, knowing when and how she was able to arrive at a "last analysis"—in her last analysis she had decided that writers hardly understood themselves, much less the people they wrote about.

She said, "That story you wrote, the first one, the one that got published—what happened when the boy asked the girl to the dance?" I told her that the girl said she'd love to go.

"Then what?"

"Then he was very glad to show her off because she was very pretty."

"But then?"

"It didn't turn out."

"Did she flirt with the other boys?"

"No."

"What did she do?"

"Worse than flirting."

"More insulting?"

"More insulting."

"Maybe she was scared. . . ."

"Maybe."

"The story—did it take place at a weekend party?"

"Yes."

"And was the boy just as glad when it was all over?"

"Yes."

"And were they both scared they'd have to go to bed together?"

"Yes."

She looked at me as if I were Tolstoi or Adlai Stevenson and she said, "I know that story. It was published in *Harper's*. I know it."

"How?"

"My teacher read it to us in Freshman English, and I had never heard a story like it before. You know, a story where nothing really happens but everything happens. . . . He read it to us and we all had to tell about it during the discussion time. That was part of his approach to education. Everybody thought the story was all about the boy and what a terrible time he was having but I said it was about the girl and what a terrible time *she* was having. I always thought that underneath you were telling that she was just as wretched as he was. I looked for the story to read myself, but I never could find that back issue of *Harper's*. And then I found it in an anthology by that fat lady. Remember the joke about the fat lady and the taxi driver? The joke where the two taxi drivers fight over which one can have the fat lady for the passenger. One calls her 'fat' and the other one says, "Don't let him insult you, 'fat lady.'""

She broke herself up laughing. The fat lady would have loved that.

After she finished laughing she said, "God, to think I'm here with you and I didn't even put your name together with the story because I never remember names like yours, but I'm so impressed. Would you like another bourbon?"

She kept staring at me, even as she was pouring.

"Did you write it on purpose," she asked, "so that you'd make people think that the girl was as miserable as the boy?"

"That was the point of the story."

"I never went to one of those college weekends. I wonder how I would have been."

"You would have been a sensation."

I was very ready to move into the take-off-your-shoes-and-pants stage, but she wanted to talk about writing.

"Did you ever write anything longer than a short story?"

"Yes."

"Then why'd you say you just write short stories?"

"I like them best."

"Why?"

"I don't know."

The two lamps in the room went off. . . . Neither of us had moved or touched anything.

"Who's your favorite writer?"

"Me."

"Besides?"

"I don't know—Nathanael West."

"I like Horace McCoy."

"So do I."

Obviously I wasn't going to be the one to bring up defective light bulbs or wiring, and she seemed to be dancing to the same tune. The lights went on again just for a moment. She was smiling to herself. Talk about smug.

I said, "Is this part of the show?"

The lights went off again. She said, "What show?"

"The good-time Charlie show?"

The lights went on.

"Charlie doesn't live here any more."

"Did he ever?"

The lights went off.

"If he did, he's gone now."

The lights went on and stayed on. She didn't pretend she hadn't been staring at me, even in the dark. Rule one turned out to be—never go into a staring contest with Nellie.

She got up and went over to the bourbon bottle and offered it to me. I declined and she poured herself another drink. When she sat down she said, "How'd you like to go to a wedding with me Sunday?"

"Whose wedding?"

"I don't know, but on Sunday we're playing a wedding in Dorchester."

"I thought you wanted to go to the beach on Sunday."

"I forgot about the wedding."

"I don't know if I can make it."

"But you said you could make the beach."

"I didn't say when."

"Well, I can only go on Sunday."

"To the wedding or the beach?"

"Obviously to the wedding—and you inferred you could come to the beach on Sunday."

"Implied."

"I think maybe you should go home now."

"I think maybe I should."

But I didn't move and neither did she. Until she got up and came over and sat on the floor, near my chair.

"You're not just nobody to me. You know, I'll never get over about you and me and the story. It's a Happening, that's what it is. Before I read that story I only read books we had at home or books at school or those ladies' magazines like *Good Housekeeping*. They all had great recipes and things for the house and ladies' stories with happy endings. It made me feel very solid and womanly to read those magazines, and it's very sad that I've lost all sense of relation to them. I mean, *Good Housekeeping* was part of my contemporary life till I heard your story, and classics are classics like bread and meat—and booze —well, that's the real thing. But when you read a story about what's happening, and it's happening when you're alive! Do you know what I mean?"

"I know . . . and thank you."

"Come to the wedding. You'll hear me sing. And there'll be lots and lots to eat and you'll get to really meet all the guys in the band and we can set things up with Saul to go to the beach the Sunday after—the Sunday after the wedding."

"My wife's coming to visit me the Sunday after."

"Tell her you're too sick for a visitation."

"I am. . . ."

"Then go home and go to bed."

And we both laughed and I told her that she could be very pretty.

"I am," she said, "you just caught me on an ugly night."

I got up to go and she said, "When you leave, go out very quietly because I'm not supposed to be screwing around. It's part of the lease—and call me at the Club tomorrow night or just come. . . . And think about the wedding and the beach."

I walked to the door. She said, "Night." I said, "Night."

And when I got to the foot of the stairs she leaned over the bannister, and in a stage whisper, she hollered, "I make it a rule not to be a first-nighter!"

I drove toward M.I.T. and to the house where the man who was thinking of a machine that would reproduce itself lived with my sister. How short-sighted, how impractical he was. Why wasn't he working on something that would accrue to all our advantages? He had a two-car garage and only one car. And I speculated as to the long-range value of his working on a car that would reproduce itself—just once, Mr. Ford.

A car was a machine. Why have a reproducing machine to make another reproducing machine? Why not a utilitarian reproductive device with no over-reproduction explosion? I could see the battlelines of logic. Dinners would be fraught with argument once I brought the car idea into the fray. My sister would assume I wanted another car so I wouldn't have to ask permission to borrow hers. She would see my proposition in terms of the fact that I couldn't sleep with her. Hah! I had never wanted to. She had large knees and elbows.

My brother-in-law would see the project as a pedestrian utilization of a major abstraction, whatever that means. Dinners would "Reek with Stark" (courtesy Ezra Pound re *Harper's Magazine*).

Once past the incestuous hump, my sister would predicate a washing machine that could reproduce other washing machines. From there we would get to oysters and pearls. A pearl that would produce an oyster, appendage-wise! We would have conversation galore unless, of course, the fool, the husband-brother-in-law fool, refused to talk back. That was his tactic. Well-schooled was he in no-speekee-dee-ingliss.

When I got home, I was greeted by my sister. She was sitting in the living room watching that prayer that ends the television day. She flipped off the set and dared me to enter her home. Not that she threw down the gauntlet. She just peeled off the average questionnaire. "Where have you been and with whom? What were you doing? Did you get sick? Do you know how much I worried? Do you know your wife—you do know you have a wife —your wife called and she wanted to speak to you and I had to tell her I didn't know where you were."

I explained that I had gone to visit a friend of a friend. It was true. Nellie was a friend of Mike's. I looked very innocent and felt more than virtuous. I had been more than virtuous. All I got was what is known as "the bad look." And all I could think was, "Christ, if I was going to get the look, I ought to get it firsthand from the wife and not secondhand from the sister."

I started toward the telephone and my sister said, "Don't call her back now, it's too late."

"Too late for what?"

"Too late to call her."

"Why did she call?"

"She wants to come up."

You tell a lie, a lie about the fact that your wife is coming to visit you the Sunday after next and there is instant retribution.

"When?"

"Weekend after this."

You see, retribution.

The pious duo, sister and wife. The sister had handled everything so beautifully that the wife had cracked. The Mountain was coming to Mohammed and the high priestess. Wasn't Cassandra a sister? The high priestess' sister was standing with bucket in hand, looking forward to washing all the sinners' feet before they violated the sanctity of her threshold.

"Look—I know that *she* didn't call *me* but that you called her, and you can tell her, next time you talk to her, that I don't believe in bed checks. And when you tell her, tell yourself, and after you tell her and yourself, add that I'm not allowed to be exposed to out-of-town company. Tell her that I'm quarantined from all non-inhabitants of Boston and environs. Tell her that I've liquidated all my insurance to invest in a company that *your* husband and I are forming. It's a company that will revolutionize the automobile industry and control men's minds."

I called Nellie the next evening. I called her at the Club. You see, I remembered her saying that she didn't want to get messages from men on her landlady's line. I told her I'd love to go to the wedding on Sunday and asked if I could come to the Club that night. She said I could come whenever I wanted to.

I ended up going every night.

The Tattletale Club. The misbegotten were thrown together, from the dish-washers on up and all the way down, and to and from me and Nellie.

Some nights I would choose to stay home and watch the late movies, and inevitably they'd get to the night-club scene and inevitably I'd get into the car and go to the Club and act it out with Nellie.

She knew all her lines and all her crosses. I decided to write a play about a man and a singer who didn't sing.

When they would call me down to the hospital for a double-check blood-check, the doctors would ask what I did with my time and how I was enjoying the city. I told them I was enjoying the best that Boston could offer. I was baby-sitting.

I would sit in the Club and drink bourbon or brandy and an occasional glass of milk or water, à la Helen Morgan. There was never any check. Nellie said it was her deal with the manager. I used to get great pleasure from watching her talk to the customers while she checked their hats and coats, and even more pleasure when she'd look at me and make faces to indicate that she thought she was far and away above this ersatz social intercourse.

She would play the same exchange of looks with the men in the band as she did with me. They were all crazy about Nellie, and when there weren't too many customers they would get the manager to let her leave her hat-check stand and come out to sing.

She explained to me that she never sang her true style because it would violate her "act." She said either you do an act or you don't, so she just sang. It was pleasant. She could carry a tune, and she was sweet. Nothing more nor less, nothing inspirational, nothing to evoke an era. At least not for me. Not then.

She knew I had my reservations and assured me it was because I hadn't heard the real thing. She had great confidence in herself, largely bolstered by Isaacs. One of the songs she sang was "Bidin' My Time." That was the only one that interested me. Because she played it totally against the saccharine Mary Martin interpretation and sang it more as if she were Lotte Lenya. I asked her why, she said, "If you don't know, why should I tell you?"

"Because I asked you."

"Take me home."

Most nights I drove her home, right to the door. Sometimes I would come up and sometimes I wouldn't. It always depended upon how she felt I felt.

She was fascinated by my ulcer and her prescription was *rest*. She would tell me that I was sick and that I ought to get off my feet. She would say, "That's what we always used to say at home. We always used to say, 'If you're sick you've just got to get off your feet and get your rest.'"

She said that she, not the Peter Bent Brigham, was the guardian of my health and welfare, both as animal and artist, and then she would stand before her door and say, "I really want you to be in shape for next Sunday at the wedding, and the Sunday after that by the sea."

In retrospect I can say that the wedding was "your average Blue Hill Avenue wedding, Boston-style," but I didn't know what I was getting into at the time. The bride either a little bit overstuffed or a little bit pregnant, and the groom terribly young, and terribly vulnerable. The parents—both the bride's and groom's—kept close tabs on the liquor vis-à-vis the checks that were pressed

61

not so surreptitiously into the blessed couple's palms, pockets and/or bosom. The bride's father was a cousin of Saul's, and Saul had given him a discount on his services. I think they threw Nellie in for good measure and she more than did her share, and more than drank her share. At one point in this elegant wedding the chanteuse tripped over the wire to the microphone and was almost, but not quite thrown into the sea of Hasidic faces.

There was more food than should, by law, be allowed in one place at one time. They had started with a cocktail reception that would, in the words of my agent, have "done Grossinger's proud," and then—with barely enough time to digest the ceremony and perhaps a furtive Bromo—they were seated before a nine-course dinner, the eating of which was interrupted only by shrieks of *appassionata* music for dancing and an occasional ballad by Nellie for kissing and counting money. Saul and the band were drinking beer, and there were twenty or thirty empty bottles rolling all around the musicians' platform.

The description of the first act of the wedding is all based on Nellie's reportage. I, myself, missed the aforesaid prelude and didn't arrive until along about the fourth course of the dinner. I introduced myself to the Greeter-Bouncer as the band's manager, and was allowed to enter.

Somebody from somebody's family greeted me with great affection, immediately assumed that my taste was the same as that of the band's, and handed me a bottle of beer. The hall was sweltering and so was I, and everything reeked with the stench of overcooked food, and I knew that if I had any kind of alcoholic beverage I would pass out, so I asked if I could have a glass of milk and at this point somebody from somebody's family almost passed out and hollered, "Saul, who's your smart friend?" and Nellie screamed, "You came, you came, I knew you would!"

They managed to sit me in a corner and I thought that I should take notes for a piece for *Commentary,* but I didn't. Instead I drank a bottle of tonic. Then Nellie asked me to dance. It goes without saying that they were playing a waltz from *The Jolson Story* and naturally she sang while we danced, "Oh, How We Danced on the Night We Were Wed."

She giggled and she hummed the rest, making fun of the words, and when we weren't bumped and pushed it was lovely dancing with her, even in that hot, rancid hall, with the smell of fat and flesh and with—yes, it was there—a certain sense of joyousness. And Nellie in her drunken haze and high as a kite and light as a feather— she really was the only person in the world who made those two metaphors come true—Nellie dancing around and around in a drunken haze saying, "Isn't it all lovely?"

The wedding didn't end. It kind of dribbled to a close and at one point the amateurs decided they'd be better than the professionals. Saul and the band and Nellie were dismissed, and I guess I was dismissed with them. We took as much beer as we could carry and loaded all the instruments into Harry's car, and Sam and Harry— they were tenor sax and drums, respectively—took some of the beer and drove off with the car. Saul and Moe and Bernie and Nellie and I started to walk toward my car drinking beer. Then we didn't walk, or rather Nellie didn't walk. She started to dance and sing. Shuffle, shuffle, step, step. Shuffle, shuffle, step, step.

> "When you're blue
> And you don't know what to do
> Why don't you just go where fashion sits

63

Puttin' on the ritz

I mean in the gutter"

The last line was done à la barbershop quartet.

Heel and toe and away we go, heel and toe and away we go. Nellie shouted, "Come on, Richard, don't be a dumb-dumb, don't be a mooncalf, you don't want to be any of those, do you? Put on the ritz with a shuffle, shuffle, step, step. . . ."

Down Blue Hill Avenue, into the gutter—shuffle, shuffle, step, step. Nellie and her wandering tribe, Nellie and the rats and mice, the children all cloak-and-suiters.

"Come on, Richard, you'll be left in the lurch and no one'll ever want you when you're old and gray."

Heel and toe and away we go.

She and Saul danced in the street until the lights of a car would threaten from over a rise and then they would scurry into the gutter and do the Fred Astaire again. . . .

> *"When you're blue*
> *And you don't know what to do*
> *Why don't you just go where fashion sits. . . ."*

Nellie screamed, "Let's go to Jack and Marion's and let's get a lot of sandwiches and go to the beach, and start the day with a swim! Please Saul, please . . . please . . . Take us, or let us go. . . ."

And Saul who was drunk and tired said, "You go."

And Nellie said, "Oh, you're too much of an angel. Just Richard and me—and you and Moe and Bernie go home. . . . Keys . . . keys-ssissimo . . . Oh, Saul. . . ."

Saul looked at me and I looked at Saul and Saul said, "My wife has the keys, Nellie. . . ."

64

So Nellie sat on the curb and started to cry, "All the wives have all the keys. . . ."

Moe and Bernie dispersed invisibly as bands are supposed to do, and Saul asked if I really wanted the keys and directions to the beach, and I told him some other time. He was pleased, because he felt that Nellie had had too much to drink and needed her rest. Then Saul disappeared.

Nellie wanted to play trained seal and balance a beer bottle on the tip of her nose, and she wanted to know why they served and drank rye whiskey, endless rye whiskey, and not scotch or bourbon at the wedding, and that launched her into a chorus of "Rye Whiskey" and then "Oh, Brandy, Leave Me Alone," and I thought to myself as I shoved her into my car that if she had never been to a college weekend, she was giving a pretty good imitation of the little girl that had been had by the Junior Class.

We got to her house and she jumped out of the car. I just sat there behind the wheel and watched her as she climbed the porch steps and started to grope around for something. I shouted, "What are you looking for?" and she motioned "Shhhhh" and then whistled that I should come up. I parked the car and stood there watching her, still groping, and I hissed, "What are you looking for?" and she said, "That's better," and kept groping, not looking, just groping. And then she said, *"Voilà!"* and handed me a key. . . .

"I never carry keys around. You don't know who might snatch your purse."

That was a lie and I told her so.

"Well, I never carry keys around if I think I might lose my purse."

I opened the door and she said, "Carry me."

"Carry you?"

65

"Carry me upstairs."

"Nellie. . . ."

"Carry me like in *Gone With the Wind* . . . and I'll give you a treat."

"Nellie. . . ."

I carried her upstairs and she had one arm around my neck and one arm free, and she unlocked the door with the one free arm, and said, "Set me down on the bed. . . ."

I set her down on the bed.

And then she said, "That was pretty rotten of you, asking for that milk."

"I'm sorry."

"You were putting them down, and they didn't deserve it."

"Sorry."

"You can be very mean."

"Sorry."

"Why don't you want me?"

"I do."

"More than what?"

"More than I should."

"Show me how much more. . . ."

And that was the climax of the wedding on Blue Hill Avenue. And the beginning of phase two.

Phase two started at five-thirty that morning when I climbed out of bed and started to get dressed and Nellie asked me where I was going. She said the john wasn't in the hall, it was right through that door on the left. I told her that I wasn't going to the john, I was going home.

"But you're in Boston. So you don't have to go home."

"Yes, I do."

"It'll spoil everything for me. You getting up like that."

66

"No, it won't. You'll go back to sleep."

"I'll never sleep."

"You'll sleep all day. . . ."

"I've never known a man who was scared of his own sister."

"Then you haven't known many men. . . ."

"That's true—but I'm learning."

"Go to sleep. I'll see you tonight."

"Give your sister my love."

"Now who's being rotten?"

"Both of us. Come here for one kiss. . . ."

"No."

"You're scared of one kiss because you know you won't go. . . ."

She opened her arms, and pulled me down to her breasts and entwined me in and out of the sheets and blankets, and she whispered, "Does she have a six o'clock bed check? Your sister?"

I remember that I slapped her, not very hard. But still and all it was a slap in the face.

And all she did was smile and pull me very close to her and say, "For that you have to make love to me again."

"For that, I don't."

"Please?"

"I'll make love to you tonight."

"Of course, tonight—but now too. . . ."

"Why?"

"Because I want to see if what I remember really happened."

"It happened."

"To which one of us?"

"Both."

"So please again."

"Twice is enough for one night."

"Count this as morning . . . if you want? I'll put all my clothes back on and let you take them all off again. Please make it happen again."

I disentangled myself from the bedsheets and from the blankets, and from her arms and legs, and I started to walk to the door. And she got out of bed. It was barely light in the room and she looked more like a silhouette than flesh and blood, and she pulled my arm from the door knob and she said, "If you don't make love to me, I'll scream for help."

"You said the landlady was deaf."

"I'll call the police and say you tried to rape me. . . ."

"They'll only try to rape you themselves."

"Richard!"

"I'll come by and see you tonight."

"Richard . . .?"

"What?" I had had enough. Why the endless pursuit and perusal of something that was done and over with?

"Richard," she whispered, "you've given me more pleasure than I've ever had in my whole life. . . ."

"How?"

She took my hands in hers and drew me to the edge of the bed. "A man can't really understand because it's physically impossible for it to happen to him, but when you make love to me—and it is love you're making to me, isn't it?—when you make love, to me, very soon after we begin I have an orgasm, and from then on until you finish I have orgasm after orgasm after orgasm, like a chain reaction, you know, or nuclear fission, or constant combustibility, and then the best is when you come . . . until a little later when I want more."

"And how was it with the others?"

"It was either awful or just okay and please let's not talk about it. Please let's talk about how it would be if we were married. I'd cook for you and proofread for you, and promise never, never to look at another man. . . ."

I went home.

Phase two was very gratifying. After all, what could be more gratifying than to have an ulcer and have someone tell you you are the most incredible lover in the world?

It was a cure-all for boredom and misery, and it was the basis for putting up with what seemed like madness and nonsense . . . it was a basis for putting up with the constant questions she asked about love and art and life in general, the prodding about who was who and who really counted to me and the constant proclamations about who was who and who really counted to and for her. She had a greed for knowledge, a belief that there were answers somewhere, and that I could produce them. Sometimes I thought she was milking my mind, and sometimes I thought she was an *idiot savant*, and sometimes I thought she was a moron.

She had a habit that I hated. She always used to sit with her dress above her knees and I used to say to her, "For God's sake, people are looking at you," and she'd answer, "But if it gives them pleasure, why shouldn't I? I mean, I give you pleasure, don't I, Mr. Hemingway?"

"Yes, you give me pleasure," said Mr. Hemingway.

"Really and truly?"

"Really and truly."

She kept bringing up the proposition that it would be divine if we were married, and that she would do everything for me, that she would even wash me like the Jap women wash their men in Japan, and I told her that it was impossible for me to consider marriage. I was not yet divorced.

She asked, "From whom? Your sister or your wife?"

I said, "Both," and I told her that I didn't know if I

wanted a divorce, and that if I did get a divorce I didn't know if I wanted to marry again. And besides, she was much younger than me.

She said she was at least ten thousand years older, and that of course I'd marry again, so why not her? She told me I could get a quickie divorce in Mexico, just like hers.

I didn't know Nellie had been married.

Mike had never mentioned it and neither had she. . . . So I said, "Mike never said you were married." She told me that there were a lot of things about her that Mike didn't know. Mostly, because she hadn't told him.

I told her he had sent me another postcard.

She was surprised and a little hurt. "That means he sent you two and he only sent me one."

"Do you want to know what it said?"

"Sure—what'd it say?"

"It said he hadn't heard from either of us, so he guessed we had found each other."

And then she smiled and arched her neck, threw her head and hair into the air, and looked way back into her heart and mind for the golden image. After a few minutes she began very slowly to speak. She told me that Mike was her dearest friend, that he was the dearest kind of friend somebody like her could have, even though she really felt that somewhere he really didn't understand anything about anything.

She said, "You know, he painted me with no face even though I was about the only face he ever saw during the whole day. I would never have done that to him . . . or, for that matter, to anybody."

When I didn't answer, she said that it was too bad that he loved all the things about her outside self but never tried really to get inside her real inside self.

"Mike loved all the glitter, all the dross. . . . I love it too, but I want to find the Pony. Horse races, you know?"

70

She said, "Maybe he was afraid to get inside me, and I can't blame him. And I still say that still and all, he's 'mine best friend.'"

Then I asked her if her husband had been a "dear friend," and she said, "A friend! Ven you got a friend that's a Hungarian, you don't need an enemy."

Not that the husband was a Hungarian or anything like that, but he was no friend of Nellie's. He was absolutely gorgeous, though, and when she and her mother found out she was pregnant they decided she'd better get married. Then she lost the baby and they decided on a divorce—she and her mother, not she and the husband. So that's how she found out all about Mexico and divorce.

"It's the weirdest thing in the world. You go down there and you feel they should *ask* you something, but they just clam up and say 'sign here' and you just get a paper—you don't even get it then, you get it later—saying that *la Señora* wife is doing something *en contra el Señor* husband because they don't have *compatibilidad de caracteres,* and the *matrimonio no existen hijos.* Then —*finito!* I used to read and read the Spanish—never the English. . . . Well, anyway, then they sent me off to college and I told you about the whole bit with Barnard and now I'm trying to convince them—them is my parents—I'm at Radcliffe and if I'm lucky I'll parlay the whole damn thing into a Ph.D."

I asked her why she never went to bed with Isaacs. She told me she never said she had and she never said she hadn't and either way it wasn't any of my business. So I pretended I wasn't interested in the whole conversation. Therefore, she couldn't resist continuing. . . . "Well, it just didn't work out that way with us. You know the way it is with you and me. I think I just amused him and needed him, and he needed me, and he was—as the poets

71

say—'neither friend nor foe'—or, as the psychiatrists say —neither friend nor father, but both. That's why I adore you. Because you're too old to be a friend or foe and too young to be a father—and too, too, too much. Make love to me.

"No! Let me make love to you, like the Japanese women do. Huh? Let me start out licking the soles of your feet. You really do have the most elegant, bony feet. I'll start just as soon as you take a bath. . . ."

She was a loving, lovely, nice, decent, mad, mixed-up, bourgeois girl. But she had the ability to make a city and a situation that were stultifying hardly stultifying. She could fill a void to a bursting point and make a pointless time seem no time at all. Good-old-time Charlie.

She poured herself into you, rather than dragging yourself out of you.

I think. . . .

She believed that the fact the subways in Boston became surface trolleys was mysterious and significant. She wanted to go up to Salem and see the Witches' Route, even though she knew it was just hooked up for the tourists. She used to sit in the Boston Common on a bench and read *Anna Karenina* and then visit the silver shop on Park Street and look for a special piece of Paul Revere silver. It was a race with her, whether or not she'd finish *Anna* or find a really good piece of Paul Revere silver first. She loved Anna Karenina—Anna, the woman, more than Anna, the book. She used to say, "What a stinking situation. I mean, Vronsky obviously isn't going to come through, and Karenin isn't going to take her back and she'll never get the kid, and, Holy Mother, is she going to do the Dutch Act!"

We rarely saw each other in the daytime. I would stay home and gestate or go down to the hospital and aggravate, and Nellie would explore the city in her own way or go to school.

She went to all the universities. She was studying Criminal Law at Harvard Law School, and Proust, Joyce, and Mann with Harry Levin at Harvard Graduate School, and Cybernetics at M.I.T. She would dress accordingly for each class and walk right in as if she belonged. She loved Harry Levin because he had never completed his Ph.D. She said that someone she had met in class had told her that he was so smart that no one could examine him for his orals. She used to long for him to notice her and pay real attention to her.

I said, "Who? The someone or Harry Levin?"

She said, "Are you just being nice or are you really being jealous? Don't tell me, let me enjoy. Saul always says, 'Nellie, all I want from life is to enjoy.' Of course it's not the someone I want to notice me. He more than notices me. It's Harry Levin. He's got the inside track on James Joyce. . . ."

Harry Levin never gave Nellie the time of day and after a while she gave up going to his classes. I told her that the Ph.D. story seemed like apocrypha and she thanked me for trying to comfort her. After a while, she stopped going to the Law School and M.I.T. as well.

She told me that being with me was an education in itself, and less "schizy" than being a non-registered nobody, when she was a bona fide mistress of somebody.

My sister didn't think Nellie was a bona fide anything, and she was even beginning to doubt that I was somebody. But her tactic was the give-him-enough-rope-and-he'll-wander-home-wagging-his-tale-and-tail-behind-him ploy. She ostentatiously opened letters from New York, ostentatiously took phone calls from New York in another room, and ostentatiously referred to people who wasted their lives in an adolescent vacuum. Whom could

73

she mean? To whom was she referring when she said that some people were incapable of marriage?

One day I went to a pay phone and I called my wife. It was like a bad play.

Wife's greeting: "How's the girl friend?"

Response: "Fine."

Wife: "Do you plan to make your permanent residence in the Commonwealth of Massachusetts?"

Response: "Maybe."

Wife: "Good."

No response.

Wife: "I've gotten a job."

Response: "As what?"

Wife: "As someone with a sense of responsibility."

Response: "To whom?"

Wife: "To the people who pay my salary."

Response: "Good for you."

Wife: "How are you feeling?"

Response: "Fine, thank you. How are you?"

Wife: "Very well, thank you."

Response: "Have you heard from Mike?"

Wife: "No, but I see Barbara."

Response: "Good."

Wife: "She sends her best."

Response: "Is she there now?"

Wife: "Yes."

Response: "Send her my love."

End of scene.

I told my sister that I would like to invite Nellie to dinner. She said, "When?" I told her as soon as possible and she said, "Wednesday." I told her Sunday would be better. Nellie didn't have to work on Sundays. My sister said, "How nice for Nellie."

I told Nellie that my sister had invited her to dinner on Sunday.

Nellie: "Why?"

Me: "Because she wants to meet you."

Nellie: "Fat chance."

Me: "Don't you want to come?"

Nellie: "Only if you want me to."

Me: "If I didn't want you, I wouldn't have invited you."

Nellie: "Who invited me? You or your sister?"

I decided to visit a monastery.

A man that I had known in the army had joined an order in Vermont. I didn't phone him to say I was coming. I just went. The "host monk" showed me my cell and let me wait. I saw my friend for one hour. For the rest of my stay he was occupied with work and/or prayer. I stayed all by myself in the cell. Promptly at five every morning a very beautiful young man used to come in and get on his hands and knees and wash the floor.

After two days I went in search of the nearest pay phone and called my agent. I told him I was coming out to California. He told me to stay where I was (he didn't know I was in a phone booth) because the picture deal was moving beautifully and that my being in such a place as Boston was very good for my image. He said it made the Producer think I was up there to do a little teaching at Harvard on the side. I asked him the side of what, and he said not to make jokes long distance collect. He said I should try to write a little. . . . Maybe a few short stories? Because after I hit very big he could sell all my old material. Look how Irwin Shaw opened up his trunks, practically selling his homework from high school!

So I went back down to Boston and told my sister that I had decided to take my own apartment.

Beginning phase three.

There's a John Garfield movie that opens with his saying, "You know how it is when you get up in the morning

75

and then the trouble starts?" In my case it was, "You know how it is when you decide to get your own apartment and then the trouble starts."

My sister exploded! To think I'd want my own apartment. Typical. She tore into my character with a devastating analysis that began with a comparison between me and the disturbed children with whom she worked. Frankly, I think my sister really had it in for me because I used to make her play doctor in the garage.

She informed me that I was no good, not worth bothering about, much less saving, and that she was going to tell the hospital that she would no longer accept any responsibility for my well-being. And that anyone that bled like I had bled and had been living like I was living, could expect to drop dead right in the middle of the street without so much as a by-your-leave. I thanked her for her good wishes and decided to write and ask my friend at the monastery to say a few for my brother-in-law.

I didn't even think of writing my wife or Mike. I knew my sister would hot-line the word directly to New York City, posthaste, top speed. It would be passed along according to priority. Mike would be the last to know. And I remember being amused at the hue and cry that would arise from my taking my own apartment. I remember thinking how Nellie would laugh at all of them . . . she would banshee-laugh at all of them.

Then suddenly I realized that, in a sense, she would be one of them. Not anything like them, but indeed one of them. . . . Of course, it would have been inconceivable to have moved her in with me.

She didn't expect me back from Vermont until Monday, so I decided to surprise her and go over to the American Legion Post where she and the band were entertaining that night. Nellie was planning to sing "You Made Me

Love You" and make each and every Legionnaire think it was for him alone. "Then," she said, "I'll run for my life. You know how immoral they are . . . both singly, and especially as a group." She had been fascinated by the fact that I planned to spend the weekend at a monastery, wanted to know all about my friend and hear everything when I got back. She had promised to spend a weekend of total contemplation and celibacy, in accordance with mine. She said, "We'll both make up for it on Monday, huh?"

I arrived at the Legion post just as she and the band were leaving, and Nellie was very down. She said she had thought it would have been fun to tease them but they were so grotesque that it had been awful instead, and Saul was mad at her for coming on like that. And Saul was right, because she had felt disgusting and felt that she had demeaned herself and the band. I made a crack about the band being pretty hard to demean, and that hurt her. She said, "Saul's doing the best he can and if it weren't for him, they'd fire me from the Club . . . so the least you can do is be nice." I told her I was always nice to Saul and she said, "I mean be nice even when you're not making points, kiddo. That's what really being nice is. . . ."

She wanted doughnuts so we went to the Mayflower Doughnut Shop on Tremont and the few people that were there stared at her. She said, "Maybe it's the dress. Maybe it's too bare—but when I sing like I like to sing it's right. . . ."

"It's not the dress . . . the dress is fine."

"I guess so. But, anyway—don't eat your doughnut. It's bad for you. Give it to me." She dunked the doughnut and ate it with great concentration. "Did you read that they're making doughnuts with stars in the middle instead of holes? It's going to ruin everything."

77

"Don't you want to hear about the monastery?"

"Sure I do—but first I wanted to get the American Legion out of my system. I'm exorcising it with doughnuts." She finished her third. "Now, tell me. . . ."

"It was very quiet."

"Were you celibate?"

"Were you?"

"Of course I was. Who was there not to be celibate with?"

"Same with me."

"Good."

"How was your friend, the monk?"

"He was fine."

"Did you talk a lot?"

"We talked for hours."

"About what?"

"Mostly about him."

"About him?"

"Yes—he wanted to talk."

"That's funny."

"Well, he had a lot of problems."

"Well, why'd he want to talk to you? Isn't he supposed to talk to the Brother Superior, or whatever?"

"He wanted to talk to me."

"Why?"

"He felt boxed in."

"Well he should—he is."

"He had a lot of conflict. . . ."

"It all sounds terribly weird to me. Why should he talk to you about *his* problems?"

"I'm his friend."

"But he's a monk."

"Well, maybe he had doubts."

"Then he should definitely not talk to you. He should talk to God. . . ."

I decided to pull out of this conversation while I was ahead. "The whole thing is very hard to explain. Let's go home."

"No, I want to hear . . . did he wear a hair shirt?"

"He didn't tell me."

"Did he have to scourge himself?"

"No, but he had to scrub floors."

"Well, they do that everywhere."

"Let's go home."

"I don't want to."

"Why?"

"I don't know. I don't think they like my having you there all the time. I think they're going to kick me out."

"Well, happy days. First you're going to get fired, now you're being evicted."

"I just feel it."

"Has anyone said anything?"

"Where—at the Club or the house?"

"Both."

"Nope—but I'm getting secret messages . . . of hostility. And I've got that feeling. . . ."

"What feeling?"

"The floundering around feeling, going-nowhere-fast feeling. . . ."

"Don't be a baby."

"I hope you gave your friend at the monastery better advice than you're giving me."

When we got to her front porch she started groping around for the keys. . . .

"Did you think you were going to lose your purse at the American Legion?"

"I might have."

"I had a feeling you might have."

"Don't worry."

"I'm not."

"Don't let's fight."

"Especially here on the front porch."

"Don't tease me."

"Shall I carry you upstairs?"

"No—but let's hurry."

When she got halfway up the stairs she turned and she smiled very suddenly for the first time all evening, and she asked me if I had ever read the *Kama Sutra*. When I told her yes, she ran up the rest of the stairs, and flung open her door and flopped on the bed.

"Teach me everything in it."

"How much have you read?"

"Only three pages . . . I couldn't bear it."

"What couldn't you bear?"

"The excitement."

"Read more."

"Now?"

"No. When you grow up."

"What's the matter with now?"

"Nothing the first pages won't cure."

"Then let's play *Kama Sutra*."

"You don't play *Kama Sutra*."

"What do you do?"

"You practice."

She had an imagination that was frighteningly akin to that period of Indian philosophy and I decided not to tell her about the new apartment just yet.

The switchover to phase three was proving more complex than I had anticipated.

One night, at the Club, Saul came over and sat down at my table. I could see the "father-of-the-girl" look in his eyes. He told me that he was worried about Nellie, and I tried to assure him that there was nothing to worry about.

"She'll survive," I said. "She'll outlive all of us."

Saul said, "Why shouldn't she?" He said, "You know we all kid her about her singing and her career, but she means it. She's good—and she's not getting a chance. . . ."

I asked him why not.

"That's a good question," he said.

"I mean," said I, suddenly righteously indignant, "if anyone can give her a chance you can."

"If anyone can give her a chance I can't."

"Why not?"

"Because I've got a family and a living to make, and like Nellie says, she's all frosting and no cake in the trade today. Nobody wants to go back and listen, everybody wants to talk so they don't have to listen. Me? I could make sounds I don't make because I have to make the sounds that they can talk by, and when I let Nellie sing, I make *her* make sounds that they can talk by. Her sound, her real sound you have to listen to. . . . Did you ever really listen to her?"

"Not really."

"Ask her sometime—ask her to sing for you. . . . It'd make her feel good. She'll do her whole act for you."

"I bet she will."

"You say you're a writer. . . . I thought writers were supposed to be interested in everything. . . . At least that's what Nellie tells me."

"She believes in the sponge theory of life. . . ."

"What's that?"

"The picking up and paying attention to and absorbing everything and everyone around you and mixing them all up and turning them into a form known as an art form. . . . It's a theory of life that nurtures an overblown imagination."

"You listen to Nellie sing. It'll make her feel good."

"Why's she feeling bad?"

"They kicked her out of her apartment. . . . It wasn't nice. They called her all kinds of names. You know, everybody thinks Boston is so hoity-toity. . . . It can be very rotten."

"Where's she going to go?"

"She'll find another place. You know my nephew is in the real estate business? You met him at the wedding. He owns a few buildings in Cambridge and he's going to give her a hand. She'll get another place in a couple—three days."

I decided not to ask Saul to ask his nephew to help me find a place too. Instead I asked some of the doctors at the hospital if they knew of a sublet. I wanted something furnished. Something I could move right into. The doctors suggested the convalescent ward. That was their idea of a joke. They told me to stay off the booze and they'd find me an apartment. "Be a nize baby, eat up all your peas and carrots and Doctor will find you a sublet—maybe even on Beacon Hill."

"Cheap?"

"Cheaper than the convalescent ward."

They were doctors so they asked me why I was leaving my sister's. I told them I couldn't work there. They gave me the doctor's equivalent of the know-it-all look. They thought I was going to move Nellie in with me. Sometimes I wonder what would have happened if I had.

All the doctors were crazy about Nellie. They thought she was enchanting, enthralling. Doctors don't get to meet Nellies except, of course, on examining tables. And whenever I came down for a series of tests, there was this wide-eyed Nellie waiting for me, wanting to know what was wrong and what was right, and what was worse and what was better. I once said to her, "Did you ever play doctor when you were a kid?" She said that was a filthy thing to ask, and then she laughed and said, "Can I take your temperature behind the cellar door?"

The doctors found me an apartment on Beacon Hill. It had two small bedrooms and a small kitchen, and a small bathroom and five flights of not so small stairs. There was a small maid, but no small butler, and I was delighted with Beacon Hill because of Oliver Wendell Holmes and all that, you know?

I thought perhaps I might even become a Gentleman-in-spite-of-myself. If Marquand could be on the best-seller list so could I, and if one of the prerequisites was Beacon Hill, I had it in the bag. The doctors said to take the stairs very slowly. In fact, they said to take everything very slowly.

The scene that followed my move—not the scene with my sister, the one with Nellie—was what television producers call the compulsory scene. I guess it was pretty lousy of me to have played it so close to the chest with Nellie. She would have said, "With me? Hah! *Against* me."

Nellie had been moved into one of Saul's nephew's apartments, on Irving Street in Cambridge, "half a block down from where e. e. cummings used to live and three blocks up from where the Polish live." It was a better deal than the first apartment. Bigger rooms, bigger kitchen, and a little porch that she could walk right out to from the bedroom. She put a cherry tomato plant out there.

The first time she visited me, she wept and said, "I think it's absolutely disgusting of you not to have said anything about your plans and not to have wanted to move in with me or have me move in with you, and if you're still a writer you must have gotten lousy 'cause you don't have any sense of the fact that I can't have a home if you're not there."

When someone like Nellie says something like that you

83

have to stop cheating and tell them the truth. I told her that I had sublet the apartment because I had had it with my sister. I had taken a sublet because I wanted to be there for as short a time as possible and that I really was a writer, and I wanted to be alone so I could write, because I "had miles to go before I slept." I thought she'd like that but she still wouldn't look at me.

I told her that I adored her but that I had to have my own life and I had to protect her against my wife and didn't want her getting involved in a lousy divorce action, and she said, "Did you decide to get a divorce?"

I hedged. And she said, "I didn't think so, so don't quote Robert Frost like it belonged to you. And don't pretend that you want to be alone so you can write, because if you really wanted to write like you can write and should write, you wouldn't have to elaborate on a Beacon Hill environment!"

She wept and said, "You know, I try not to drink too much around you because I know it's temptation and it's bad for your stomach lining, but if you don't care like that about me, then I don't care like that about you, so I'm going to do whatever I want which will include seeing that you drop dead."

And then she pulled herself together and she lit a cigarette and took two drags and started to put it out. But she stopped and gave me one of those stares, and she said, "Stick out your hand. I'm going to put this cigarette out right on your hand. Come on! Stick out your hand! Palm down!"

So I did. . . . And I waited. . . .

But she pulled back, and put the cigarette out in a wet ashtray.

After a while she said, "I was never allowed to smoke when I was a kid and I used to have to do it in secret places. Once I was smoking with this boy in my school and he teased me about being afraid to smoke in public. I took my cigarette and put it out on his hand. He was the one I married. You know what he told me? That when I burned his hand like that he knew that I was a pushover. The one I married. You know what he did to me? He told me that everybody was sleeping with everybody and so I went to bed with him, because I used to want to be like everybody and I knew I wasn't. I knew I was special, and I knew I was different from the rest of them—I mean, you know, the other kids at school. And I knew that I had to do things that they didn't have to do, and that I had to do things that would make my parents proud of me. And that's why it's so terrific that my parents think I'm at Radcliffe. I'm sure they're telling everybody at home."

I asked her where home was and she said, "Home is where the heart is," and took a stance like the Statue of Liberty, and I told her that Mike Isaacs had written me that she had never told him where her home was, and she said, "He never asked me." So I said, "I'm asking you," and she said, "I'm not telling you," and I said, "Why?" and she said, "Because," and then as only she could do, she threw her arms around me and clung to me and said, "Let's play house."

Nellie kept hatchecking for the Tattletale and I kept serving as occasional guinea pig for Peter Bent Brigham, and life was very much the same except we had almost, but not quite, changed our locale from her place to mine. She loved my place even though, as she said, it was "her enemy."

She never asked for a key and I never gave her one. Maybe I should have wrapped one up in tissue paper and tied it with a ribbon and said, "Here—you happy?" But I never did.

Nellie was right about me and the writing. I tried to write, but I couldn't.

I decided the next best thing was to read. I read the collected short stories of Conrad Aiken, and I began to see Boston through his eyes. The place was one big hospital-graveyard and all the women, professional or not, were nurses.

I discussed the hospital-graveyard theory with Nellie and she thought I was all wrong. She said it wasn't that Boston was a hospital or a graveyard, it was that Conrad Aiken felt like a corpse.

Then one night, just as I was leaving to pick her up at the Club, my agent called to say that the picture deal looked very hot, very hot indeed. I was delighted to hear from him. It was a first. The first time he called me, not me him.

I asked him how hot "very hot indeed" was and he said things were "hot and how," not definite, but hot and he would keep in touch. He asked me how my teaching was coming along. Some people get an idea into their heads and nurture it. I told him Harvard was giving me a Chair, and he said, "A what?" and I told him to call me as soon as he knew things were hot enough to "be set."

That night I went to the Club and told Nellie I had a good chance to go to the Coast. Of course she asked, "The coast of what?"

I explained and she said, "But I want you to be a writer-writer, not a movie-writer." I told her that if the price was right, I'd be a movie-writer.

She said, "But I want you to be a writer of great books. You told me you once wrote a book."

"Did I?"

"You know you did."

"It was an eminently unsuccessful book. Distinguished, but eminently off the best-seller list."

And she said, "Aren't they the best kind?"

I told her I didn't know any more. Then she said, "Let's get Saul to give us a bottle wholesale, and walk all the way home to my place. Let's get a bottle of bourbon. I'm all out."

I asked Saul to get us a bottle of bourbon and he looked at Nellie and he looked at me and then he looked back at her, and if I didn't bleed he did—a little.

We walked and we drank and Nellie loved to stand beside a tree and hide behind a postbox and take a belt. We walked and she said, "You know—if you hadn't moved out of your sister's we couldn't have this great walk because you'd have her car."

She looked over Cottage Farm Bridge down into the depths of the river and said, "California is the most mechanized state in the world . . . when you go out there everybody has a car—or two, or three. Even the kids—I read that."

We walked through Harvard Square and weaved in and out all the statues, and we passed that funny gray house she used to live in, and walked into the funny gray house she had moved into—the house just half a block from where e. e. cummings used to live. . . . We got to the door and she took another slug of bourbon.

"I used to drink champagne," she said, "and here I am back to bourbon. However, I do think it's very much in the American tradition. And plays against my style, which is essentially European."

We had seen a revival of *The Barefoot Contessa* the Sunday before and I guess she was playing Ava Gardner to the hilt. She acted devil-may-care, nothing means anything. She said that she thought her singing was a secondary talent as far as she was concerned and that acting —straight drama—was her true talent. She could be anybody, she was anybody, because she wasn't anybody. We

87

got to her door. She got her key, and said, "You can go home now."

And I told her to come off it.

She pushed me, like a nasty kid pushes another nasty kid. I played the part of the other nasty kid, and I pushed her back. She fell against the door, and stood up and spread her arms wide.

She said, "You're not at all what I thought you were."

"Or what you wanted me to be?"

"Go 'way."

"I'm going to go away, but not now."

"Rubbing it in?"

"No—just stating a fact."

She looked up at me, begging to be victimized. And I thought, if that's the game she wants to play that's the way we'll play it. So I wrested the key from her hand and unlocked her door and pushed her into the hall and up the stairs, and into her room, and I forced myself on her.

I pretended to rape her and she pretended that she had been raped.

Later she told me she thought the whole thing had been an Absolute Gas.

Nellie.

Who was Nellie? The purist who believed that writers should be real writers, or the hoyden who had to pretend that she had been ravaged?

We sat in the dark and smoked, and she said, "If you're going to prostitute what you have to give me, I'll prostitute what I have to give you . . . but just the part I have to give you. Never my real self."

And then she came and sat on my lap and took my face in her hands and said, "That's a lie, because I have everything to give you . . . and I just can't figure out what you want. You know what I mean? I mean, if I'm going to sacrifice myself it really ought to be for something that's essentially worthwhile. No?"

I told her yes.

"You'd really rather write than go to the Coast?"

"Of course."

"Hey Richard?"

"What?"

"Lie some more. . . ."

I think Nellie must have understood that I was almost never anything but honest with her. She had taken me on my own terms just the way she had taken Mike on his, just the way she had taken the boy she had burned with a cigarette and married. Then why was I different?

Nellie would have said, "You weren't different. I was. . . ."

She'd been right about being evicted, and inevitably, she was right about being fired. Inevitably, she lost one job, and inevitably she got another. I remember the week that she was looking, she said, "Talk about Conrad Aiken, I know everything there is to know about Boston because when you look for a job you just get to go everywhere, and let me tell you—there's a far cry from the first floor of a building to what it's like upstairs."

She burst into my apartment one afternoon and announced that she had gotten a job at the Woman's Exchange, and her reaction was, "Isn't that marvelous? It sounds like a whorehouse. But it's really not. It's really a Thrift Shop, and people make things or they bring rummage and then they sell them to the same women that are making things and bringing rummage. It's an interesting insight into our economy, isn't it? God, I wish I were a Communist, but you know, I never can be, because I love the flag. Isn't that terrible? I really do dig it. I really dig the flag. I remember during the Second

World War—I was very little then—we used to have to stand up at the movies when they played 'The Star-Spangled Banner' and I cried every time. But this job at the Woman's Exchange is very nice and very respectable, and they're giving me forty-five dollars a week, and so now we can have all our nights together."

I lowered the boom on my flag-loving patriot and I told her that my agent had called to say the picture was set and that the doctors were going to give me the final checkup, and that I was leaving for California in a week.

And she said, "Is the price right?" And I told her that it seemed very right, and she said, "Well, I guess if the price is right you buy the ticket—and you get off wheh duh money is, Amos."

She said that if this were a movie musical—"You know, like a Doris Day one, or like those old Dick Powell ones that you see on *The Late Show*, you would be the man and you would sing, 'California, Here I Come' but you're not coming, you're going, so I'll sing the girl's song instead, okay?"

And I said, "Fine," and she sang

> *"Don't ever leave me,*
> *Now that you're here*
> *Here is where you belong.*
> *Ev'rything seems so right when you're near,*
> *When you are gone, it's all wrong.*
> *I'm so dependent*
> *When I'm in trouble . . .*
> *It's you that I run to*
> *So-ooo-*
> *Don't ever leave me*
> *'Cause if you do,*
> *I'll have no one*
> *To run to. . . .*

"Of course, I don't have the lyrics right, but you don't have to and I like them better my way than the real way. That was my best Helen Morgan," and then she laughed and said, "That's like saying that's my best dress."

And then she began to cry, but it was a strange kind of cry, a gagging kind of cry. She said, "It's that song, that stupid song. It's part of my act and I always think of how lousy it was for Helen Morgan with that married man she hung around with and everything, and how lucky I am not to need anybody."

I asked her if it was like the flag and "The Star-Spangled Banner," and she said, "Kind of like, but not really."

I had never believed Mike and Saul when they told me about Nellie's singing. I used to think there was a weakness in that she sang from the throat and not from the diaphragm, but I was wrong. She sang from the thought, not the diaphragm.

What was she to Helen Morgan or Helen Morgan to me that I should weep for them? Maybe I've got the lyrics wrong, but I like them that way.

I checked into the hospital for that final checkup and Nellie moved right in with me. God knows how she did it. She would come and visit and then stay overnight. I've never heard of anyone beating the visiting rules rap, especially the overnight visiting rules rap. But Nellie beat it. She would hide in a closet or a ladies' room, and when everyone had left she'd sneak out of her hiding-place and come to my room and laugh like a banshee. At one point she told me that she was sleeping with the head resident and the head floor nurse, and blackmailing both of them, and that's how they let her stay. I knew she was lying, but I loved it when she said she thought of herself as a medical Mata Hari . . . seducing the staff to get to the patient.

She would bring me French vanilla ice cream and caviar and she would bring bourbon—for herself only, off bounds for me—and pound cake, and she bemoaned the fact that she couldn't sneak it into the floor kitchen and toast it because she thought that toasted pound cake with butter was the absolute end.

I never asked her where she got all the food. I knew that her salary from the Woman's Exchange did not encompass beluga caviar. Then one day she explained that she was a thief, a real thief, a crook, a Raffles, a Robin Hood, because she only stole from the rich.

"I steal from the chain stores because they're stealing from us. I never steal from real little stores because they don't have a big markup and the chain stores do. I don't know, really. Maybe I don't steal from the real little stores because the people are real. The people in the chain stores aren't real. When I was living near Columbia —you know, when I was with Mike—I would steal salamis and Nova Scotia salmon. They sliced that Nova Scotia and they put it in cellophane packages already weighed, and I'd steal the cream cheese to go with it. Once I stole a five-pound salami. I just slipped it up my sleeve, and then I got Swiss cheese to go with it and rye bread, and for days we ate so great!" With great nostalgia, she repeated, "We ate so great. . . . But I guess that really half the fun of the eating was the stealing, and I love you better than salami or Swiss cheese. And my dear, dear heart, when a man gets a woman to put a brick of French vanilla ice cream inside her blouse, that's true love."

I guess I never really will know what shape my stomach is in. I had Nova Scotia and salami and French vanilla and beluga caviar, and Nellie in my bed, and how do you judge a medical work-up without taking those factors into consideration? She called it, "Our honey-moon in the hospital. Bless this home."

God knows what they found, but they let me out and said, "Watch your diet," in words of more than one syllable.

She was there to take me home. I left which home up to her. She had gotten the cab so the address was her choice. She took me back to my apartment—not hers. We were walking up the stairs and she told me that one of the reasons I made such a good showing on the tests was because of her visits, that she had read a magazine that there was scientific proof that when mothers were allowed to stay over in hospitals with babies the babies got better faster. I didn't appreciate the comparison, but it gave her a great deal of pleasure to think that she had outfoxed the doctors.

That night we ate stolen caviar and drank a bottle of champagne, and made love, and she never said a word about the fact that I was leaving in the morning, and that I was already packed. She never asked what I was going to do with my apartment, where I was going to be staying in California, or how long I was going to be staying in California.

I was catching an early plane for New York. I was going to stop by and see Mike, and my wife. And Nellie had to go to work at the Woman's Exchange, so we left the apartment early in the morning. And she told me to be absolutely sure to give Mike her eternal love and to ask him if he knew where her face was. And I told her I would write her when I knew where I was going to live, how long I was going to be there, what the whole situation was. And then she said, "We're crossing the threshold on the way out! Carry me over backwards."

When I set her down she said,

                Buffalo Bill's
                defunct
                          who used to
                          ride a watersmooth-silver
                                              stallion
                and break onetwothreefourfive pigeonsjustlikethat
                                                        Jesus

                he was a handsome man
                                    and what i want to know is
                how do you like your blueeyed boy
                Mister Death

She told me her neighbor, mr. e. e. cummings, wrote
that and that it had no punctuation so you could say it
any way you wanted to but you had to get the lyrics
right.

The Agent

My name is Nat Gench. I'm an agent.

Not mentioning any names, I'm not the type of agent that a certain agent who had a certain client who died in a certain way that a lot of people think was a little mysterious, is.

I don't want anything for myself out of this. My interest is purely personal. Whatever grief I'm suffering I'm keeping to myself.

I'm not asking or taking anything from anybody, and I'm not expecting to get it.

All I want is to set the record straight about who's who and what's what and let a little truth come out in the middle of a lot of lies and then let it be over with, like Nellie, she should rest in peace.

I'm not out to exploit anything or anybody, and if I'm talking it's not to hurt anybody—if the truth hurts, whoever's being hurt deserves to be hurt. At least that's what I think.

Because I never sold Nellie or anybody else short, and God should strike me dead if I would do that especially now. Nellie would be the first one to agree with me. Nellie would be the first one to tell you just how much I did for her, and she would be the first one to tell you that she knew I would always be grateful to her for what she did for me, and she would be the first one to say that if there was anyone she could have come to with her troubles—whatever they were—that one should have been me because I would have moved Heaven and Earth for her. And wherever she is, if she knew how certain decent people were suffering from what she did, she would be sorry and she would know that what she did was wrong. That, I can swear to. It's like all kids today. They have everything a person could want, so they don't want it. They're miserable to themselves and to other people. And when they hurt you, they're sorry too late to make up for it.

My own kids are like that in some ways.

But killing yourself, that's something different. And of all people to kill themselves, I never really thought it would be Nellie.

So when I found out she killed herself, I said to everybody—they must have the wrong person.

And when I found out they didn't have the wrong person I didn't say anything. I just sat and I asked myself what is it that we do to people, or that people do to us when we're here today and gone tomorrow anyway? And if God says here's a piece of cake, take a bite, you should eat the whole piece and not ask any questions.

I'm the only one that took Nellie for what she was. I could see she was a good person. Right from the beginning we hit it off. Right from the time she walked in my office, out of nowhere, with nothing but a valise.

Because I'm the kind of person that likes things organized, I like to start my day with a little headstart, so I get into the office early. I don't mean that I'm there before nine just to see if the secretaries are getting in on time. I just like to get there early for myself. That way I know I'm one step ahead of myself.

I have a problem sleeping. I go to sleep late and I get up at six o'clock in the morning. My wife tells me it's nothing to worry about. She tells me it's just that I'm one of those people who need less sleep than other people. She doesn't have an answer to the fact that I take two sleeping pills and a half a glass of whiskey and I stare at the wall, and when I finish staring at the wall and fall asleep, it's only for four hours when anybody else would be knocked out for twelve. For everything else my wife has answers, but not for the four hours. But, who's going to change things?

It was one morning about a quarter of nine that this girl walked into my office carrying a valise and wearing what I would call traveling clothes. She said, "I want to see the head agent." I said, "I'm the head agent," and she said, "Amos Agent, take a look at Stella Star." I looked and I said, "Girlie, what's your name?" She said, "Cynthia Stardust." Being very polite, I said, "Look, Miss Stardust, come in when the office is open and ask for an appointment because I don't see anyone except by appointment." She said, "But you're seeing me. There's nobody here but you and me, so you're seeing me. So we're having an appointment, see?" That was a good point, so I said, "All right. I'm seeing you. Have a seat."

She said, "You're Richard's agent, aren't you?"

"Richard who?"

"My Richard's."

"Who's your Richard?"

"Your Richard."

Games yet? All I needed after four hours' sleep.

"Which of my Richards is your Richard?"

"Guess. . . ."

So I guessed. "Condon? Burton? Brooks? Chamberlain?"

She didn't choose, so I chose.

"Nixon, maybe?"

She said, "I'll take Condon. He has the most staying power. As a writer, that is." She said, "That's a joke, son." I got right away what she meant, so I told her I once handled Kenny Delmar. She was very impressed.

She said, "He was Senator Claghorn, right?" And I asked her how she knew about Senator Claghorn and she said she knew all about Senator Claghorn and Allen's Alley from when she found *Treadmill* in an apartment she had once sublet in Boston, and that she had shown it to Richard and that they both read it together, and that Richard—the real Richard—was Richard Timon, the writer, and that she knew I was his agent because he used to worry about me more than anyone.

"Never about you as a person," she said, "just about you as his agent. He always worried about your not working hard enough for him. But I told him that since what you made was solely dependent on what *he* made you'd rather do right by him than be President."

I said, "President of what?" and she said, "You're really going to be a gorgeous agent. You're so flat."

Then she laughed and said, "You really don't have all those other Richards, do you? The famous ones?" So I told her I really didn't, but I could have, and then she said, "Maybe you still will. I mean Richard—my Richard —told me people are forever changing agents. Especially

98

after they get rich. And famous. They change agents. That's disgusting, isn't it?"

I could see that she talked my language so I settled back to listen. She told me how she had known Dick Timon from Boston and that's how she knew I was his agent, and so when she decided to come to California she decided that if I was good enough for Timon, I was good enough for her. Then she asked me how he was, and where he was, and how he was doing, and she threw it out, very off-the-cuff, very offhand, and I'm a guy that knows a little bit, so I said, "He didn't write to you?" and she said, "I guess not—but he's not that style. Do you smoke?"

I told her I smoke. And she said, "Cigarettes?" and I said, "Cigars." And she made like she was a cigarette girl and had a tray on her, and she said, "Tiparillos?" I gave her a cigar and she lit it, and then she said, "Boy, this is really Hollywood, *n'est-ce pas?* Well, tell me now, about Richard."

So I filled her in, adding a little here and there, taking a lot away here and there. She ate it up. I could tell I was telling her about the Somebody who's the real Somebody. When I finished she said, "Thank you." And when I didn't say anything back she said, "I had an abortion."

As my wife would say, that was when I should have stuck my toe out, not in. But I didn't.

She said, "Doesn't everybody . . . ? Have an abortion? I mean, you've got to figure that for every abortionist, there are a hell of a lot of abortionees. But look, don't tell anybody. I mean, it's not the kind of thing you want to get around. Don't you think?"

The first thing I thought of was, "I'm glad I'm not her father," and the second thing I thought of was, "So where is her father?" So I asked her and she said, "I don't have a father."

So I asked her where was her mother. She said, "I don't have a mother either. I just sprang like Minerva from the head of Zeus. That's mythology. You know, mythology, like Bulfinch?"

Being an agent I know that there are times just to admit you don't know. So I said, "Which Bulfinch?" And she said, "God, am I going to have to teach you to read?" And I told her I read what came across my desk, so she said, "You really need me. Culture-wise."

Remember Gail Russell? Probably not. . . . I remember Gail Russell because she was somebody who I didn't handle. She was a beautiful girl who had a beautiful chance to make it. And maybe if I had been smart I would have looked at Gail Russell and said, "I'll handle you," and she would have had someone like me to give her a hand. But I figured that she was doing okay without me and I was doing okay without her, and while I liked her as a person, I could smell trouble. She was a medium-sized big-star who always was the one that was going to get it in the suspense stories. The road-company version of Joan Fontaine in *Rebecca*.

And when they found dead Gail Russell in the lousy room with all the pills and all the empty vodka bottles and she was all puffed up, I thought to myself that it was such a waste of what would have been such a girl, and I felt very bad.

And I'm not saying that I'm second-guessing about Nellie, now when it's all over in a different way, but I'm saying that maybe—a little bit because of Gail Russell and a little bit because I smelled vodka on her breath—Nellie's—before nine o'clock in the morning, I decided to take her on.

Just to look at, she was just another one that comes out here, very pretty, nice figure, very anxious to please whoever and whatever, and pretending she didn't want too much, but wanting everything and not fooling anybody.

I could have slotted Nellie right in that girlie category because I needed ten percent of her aggravation like I needed a hernia operation. But she was sending me messages. Ask me to explain and I can't. It's a feeling you either get or you don't. Like the guy—if there is one—who saw Turner, in that sweater in the drugstore. A Hollywood folktale.

Sometimes I think I took Nellie on because I was selfish and I knew I had a winner in Timon, and I knew that Nellie was going to make waves with him. And I figured if I could keep an eye on her, I would maybe be able to stop the trouble. Let me tell you, Timon had enough without Nellie thrown in.

Nellie asked me if his picture had been a success. I told her that they hadn't put another writer on yet, which gave her a general idea of how he was starting to be a success. And she said, "Well? Are you going to sign me up?" So I said, "As what?"

She told me that she was a singer and that she had worked out this nightclub act from the twenties that had a lot of class and that really swanky people would go for. I explained that classy acts for swanky people weren't selling. She said that in some ways the act didn't have to be just for swanky people, and then she gave me her bit about Helen Morgan-Ruth Etting. And I told her it would be easier to book a human trapeze.

So she said, "Okay—then get me on television or maybe even in the real movies. Groom me as a starlet. In the tradition. You know, fix me up and sell me." She pretended to come on very sexy. "I'll wear false eyelashes and falsies. Isn't that what they do? And you can get me all the publicity, and the parties. And I'll be window dressing. And then someday we'll get a flukie break and I'll sing in my real style—and it'll make all the columns—and I'll be a fad. You want to try it? Huh? I'm willing if you are, but my only problem is I won't be able to sleep with anybody for a while because you're not supposed to and you're not in the mood after an abortion."

She had to zing that zinger in just to make sure she was letting me know I wasn't going to get off the hook without aggravation.

But I signed her.

I signed her and then I told her I should have my head examined. She assured me she'd pay off very big.

And she did. You should only know how big. But I'm not opening my books to anybody but the accountant.

Anyway, there I was with Nellie on my list and it was only twenty minutes after nine, and already I was exhausted.

The girls started coming in, and the phone started ringing, and the calls were coming in from New York because of the time difference, so Nellie said, "Well, I guess I better go now." I said that was a good idea and she said, "Oh, listen. . . ." long pause. She said, "Listen, do you know a good place to live? I was kind of thinking of the Garden of Allah because of F. Scott Fitzgerald and Thomas Wolfe. . . . But I guess being an agent and reading only what comes across your desk. . . ."

See, she never forgot anything.

"Being an agent you don't know the famous letter that Thomas Wolfe sent to F. Scott Fitzgerald, 'Dear Scott, is there really such a place as the Garden of Allah?' "

I told her that being an agent, I didn't know about the letter, but I did know that they had torn down the Garden of Allah, and that it would have been too expensive anyway. Then I told her to ask the receptionist where a nice decent place for a single girl to live would be.

Nellie thought that was very funny. She said, "I know what you're thinking. You're thinking I'll get in trouble and have to have another abortion."

I told her I wasn't exactly thinking of it in those terms, but as long as she had brought the subject up she should watch herself. She laughed and said, "Don't worry, I will."

Then she got serious. She started playing with her dead cigar and I waited for her to tell me what she wanted to tell me and she said, "I'm not going to call Richard because I don't want him to think I followed him out here or anything. But it's obvious that you're going to call him, so make it seem that your bumping into me was very casual. Like you discovered me, maybe? And don't tell him the gory details, just kind of drop the fact that you're handling me, and when I get my decent place to live I'll give you my address and then if Richard wants it you can always give it to him. Right?"

I said, "Right."

Then she said, "Could I have a hundred dollars? I mean, just till we get things rolling with me, and then I'll pay you back. You can deduct it from my earnings. I know a hundred seems like a lot but I've got a cab waiting downstairs with my trunk in it, and it's going to be a fortune."

I told her to go into the lobby and talk to the receptionist about places to look for rooms, and I sent one of the kids down to see if the cabby was still waiting. He was there, so the kid told him to wait a little more, trunk and all. Elsie, my receptionist, gave Nellie a few leads and I gave her the hundred and she walked out the door and in two seconds she came running back. She said,

"Christ, I forgot my suitcase. That's good luck. It means I'll be coming back. . . . I mean, according to Freud it does."

Elsie is a very funny girl and she said, "What are you going to do for an encore, boss?"

I went into my office and I called my wife and I asked her how things were going and if the kids were okay. She thought I was crazy. She said, "You just walked out of this house an hour ago, so what are you asking me if the kids are okay for?" And I told her that sometimes something happened to make you nervous, but as long as everything was okay I was okay too, and I told her that she should have a nice day. She said the same back to me. Which was very nice, our both wishing each other a nice day. And let me tell you, I should have a nice day like she was going to have a nice day. When my wife reaches out to light a cigarette it's a major effort. Not that she's lazy or a shirker—but she has a nice little Jewish man to take care of her, and let me tell you, I wish I had a nice little Jewish man to take care of me.

I'm not saying I resent anything, and there's nobody that's a mother like my wife, and a hostess. She has what is known in her circles as the domestic-executive ability. She can figure more ways to hire help and keep them working than Jimmy Hoffa. And she treats them very nice—God bless her.

After I talked to my wife I called Dick Timon. Like Nellie said, it was obvious I was going to do it.

I said, "A very nice girl just left my office, and she told me that she knew from Boston that I was your agent, and that I should casually mention that she was in town."

And he said, "When'd she get here?"

I told him, like twenty minutes ago, and I had a feeling that I was her first stop. And he said, "Who's going to be her second stop?"

I told him not to worry, that I didn't tell her his address.

So he, being Timon, said, "Or phone number?"

So I, being me and tired already, said, "Or phone number."

And then he asked me how come she didn't ask for his address or his phone number like he was offended.

I said, "I think maybe she just has nice manners."

And with such love in his voice he says to me, "Nellie."

And with no love in my voice, I told him it was very nice that he remembered her name.

He said, "Listen, Nat, this is too complicated to explain now. . . ."

That he didn't have to explain to me.

He said, "It's a long story. Someday I'll tell it to you. But if she asks you if you talked to me just make sure to tell her I had to go out of town for a while."

So I said, "She came out here just to see you."

He said, "Get her a job. She has interesting qualities."

I told him getting jobs for people with interesting qualities was not so easy.

He said, "That's your problem, not mine."

Then he told me again to make sure not to let her know where he was for a while because he had his own problems. He didn't have problems. He had A Problem. She was one of those Italians they bring in for a Bible picture. He moved her in with him out at Malibu and at first it was a very hot thing and then it got cooler, and I think she was like halfway on her way out, but I think he was not quite finished and wanted her to stay till the end of the picture. His picture, not hers.

So I asked him how he was doing with his Italian and he said, "*Come si dice* bored *in Italiano?*"

I said, "Your accent stinks."

He said, "Which one?"

105

• • •

Let me tell you, people always put down agents. They think scientists and politicians and doctors are great, and they think to be an agent is to be a nothing. But take a client and make them into something—it's like making the Bomb. Give me a Ph.D. I'll be a scientist.

Nellie got a place in one of the places that the girl in my office told her about. And she became what is known as part of the girl system. One girl tells another girl to tell another girl where to live. And soon a lot of girls all live in the same place and they all become best friends and steal each other's boyfriend.

This place my girl told Nellie about was an apartment building near Laurel Canyon where she could have a room and a kitchenette and they had a patio with a swimming pool, and it was cheap maybe a hundred . . . a hundred and twenty-five dollars . . . but it was clean and nice. They get a living room where they sleep and a kitchenette, and they all flip over the idea that they've got a swimming pool, and I'd like to have a dollar for every time they don't go in swimming. They sit there and they lie to each other about who they're sleeping with, and who they're planning to sleep with, and who wants to sleep with them. They all watch Jack La Lanne so they can be firm. Go have a daughter and you'll understand why I worry about these things.

As soon as she got settled she started calling me. Hotline Nellie. She called on the average of twenty times a day, and finally to clear the lines I set up a date with her so she could sing for me.

She came in wearing a camel's-hair coat and one of those long black *schmatas* they used to call evening gowns. In the middle of the day, yet. If you know California you'll know she was lucky she didn't get stopped for being peculiar. Then she went into the audition room where I had the piano and she explained that she should have a piano player but since she didn't want me to go to any trouble to get a piano player for her she would play herself but that I should remember that she wouldn't be able to do her gestures. Gestures, yet?

I sat in a chair and she sat down at the piano and she started to feel it out, like to see what she could get out of it. She went at the piano like she was romancing it, and I'm a guy that knows a little about music and I could see that she knew exactly where she was going. She had a plan for that piano. She was a great one for plans for everything. And then she started to sing and, God bless her, the dress and all, she took me back to the time when guys like me used to go crazy for singers and want to support them. She sang "Why Was I Born?" and then she belted "Shakin' the Blues Away," and then she did "Shine On Harvest Moon" and "Out in the Cold Again," and then she asked me if that was enough. She said she didn't want to do her whole act because it was a stand-up act and it couldn't be done if you had to play the piano, and I told her that what I heard was enough and that I liked it very much, and she said, "Thank you."

So I said, "No. Thank *you*."

And she said, "You're very welcome." And she waited for what I was going to say next.

I said I thought what she did was very good and very special. She said, "So?" And I said, "So it's a little too special for right away. And I'd like to sell you a little straighter for now. You know—like with a guitar."

She got just what I had in mind. She knew I was figuring to get her a job in a coffee house to see how she handled herself, and how she went over with the kids.

She knew, and she didn't like it.

I explained to her that we had to see how she went over as a performer in general and as a personality, and even just as a person. That made her mad.

She said, "I'm not *just* a person. And neither are you. You liked what I did. So why denigrate both of us?"

I didn't answer.

She said, "I didn't know what denigrate meant either until Richard told me. It means insulting someone in a very low way."

I gave her a look and she gave me a look, and she said, "Richard's an expert on vocabulary."

I said, "Among other things." So she dropped the subject and said, "I think it's disgusting that I have to make the whole guitar thing with a low register just to find out whether or not people like me *just* as a person."

What was I going to say? "That's show business"? or "I can sell a girl with a guitar, but not one with a black *schmata*"?

So I sat and I tried to tell her that life wasn't like the old movies where the pretty girl singer with a heart gets featured in a supper club where people come in evening gowns to drink and hold hands and dance, and where they stop everything when the girl singer comes on with the gusty sound. What was I going to tell her? That she was born in the wrong time. That if she was born twenty-five or thirty years ago—or maybe (because, like they say, things go in circles)—maybe twenty—thirty years from now she would be in style.

I liked her style. I liked what she was doing. I could see she was soft-and-sweet and hard-and-controlled at the same time. I liked the fact that she didn't sing songs with messages that told you to lay down in the street. She was a private singer. She was the kind of singer that could sing "Just One of Those Things." When the singer who can sing it sings "Just One of Those Things" they can let go with everything but never really let you know what "just one of those things" was. That's hard to understand unless you understand Music.

But what I liked and what she liked wasn't going to get her a job, and a job was what she needed, and I knew a guy who owned one of those coffee houses where they have folk singers, and he owed me a favor. I didn't put it to him like he owed me a favor, I put it to him like I was doing him a favor. And he put it to me that my little singer would have to do a little waiting on tables between singing. So I told Nellie and I told her the money would be nice for a start, and she said, "Promise me it'll just be a start."

I said, "Sure, sure—just a start," and she said, "I'm a lemon, aren't I?"

I told her not to talk like that and she asked me if I knew the song:

> *"Girls can never change their nature*
> *That is far beyond their reach.*
> *Some girls are born a lemon*
> *And some are born to be a peach.*
> *But the law of compensation*
> *Is a law I always preach.*
> *You can always squeeze a lemon . . .*
> *But just try and squeeze a peach."*

I told her I didn't know the song but would she write the words down for me for future reference.

And then she came right out of the bad mood and she said, "I really adore you and we're going to really get places. Both of us. And it's terribly exciting to think of someone like you owning ten percent of me. It's like I'm a white slave. Do you know about white slavery? Like with Bugsy Siegel out here and that whole bunch?"

I told her I had heard a little bit about it a couple of years ago.

She said, "My mother told me all about white slavery. She warned me that when I went to New York I should be very careful watching out *not* for men, but for old ladies. Especially in elevators, because those old ladies look just like grandmothers and they get behind you and stick a hypodermic right into your behind that's full of dope, and it works instantaneously and you start to have a fainting fit and the old lady pretends she's your grandmother and she tells the people in the store to let her take you out of the elevator, and she takes you away and you're never heard from again because you're a white slave."

She told me, "The funny part of the whole story is that I never understood that a white slave was going to have to be a prostitute. I always thought Mama meant that you were going to have to be a maid, that you'd have to wash dishes and make beds and all that. So let me tell you, did I watch out for those old ladies!"

I think Nellie was the only girl that ever came to California who thought a white slave was a maid. But the white slave part wasn't what interested me. It was the mother part. I said to her, "I thought you told me you didn't have a mother," and she said that it was very complicated and that sometime she'd tell me about it, but not now.

I said, "You know, you either have a mother or you don't have a mother," and she said, "There are seven levels of ambiguity—vis-à-vis perception." That shut me up.

So she said, "It's in a book. A book by Empson. After you read Bulfinch on Mythology, read Empson on Ambiguity." And that is when I got to know that with Nellie, you didn't ask questions.

She thought that even though it was lower than being

a real white slave, she was willing to take the job at the coffee house, but she made me promise that I'd let her go around and audition her real act for people in her own way. And she said, "If you don't promise—I'll do it anyhow, so promise and you'll be in on it. I'll really work on it and I won't shame you. I've got plans. . . ."

She felt that since her Helen Morgan bit hadn't worked in Boston it definitely didn't have a chance in L.A., so she was going to push Ruth Etting. Not Doris Day's version of Ruth Etting. She thought that was cheap. The *real* Ruth Etting was never sentimental but was high and soprano like Morgan, but with a touch of down and dirty.

"It's the difference between being so desperate about one guy that you have to give *all* the fellows a break like Helen Morgan, and being crazy about one rotten gangster like Etting was. You know what I mean?" I knew what she meant. I didn't know if she knew what she meant, but I knew.

She asked me how she should dress for Ruth Etting, and I said, "Dress the way you dress for Helen Morgan. No one will know the difference." She said, "In these tatty old clothes?" and I said, "How much are you going to hit me for this time?" and she said, "Another hundred?"

Then she said, "Hey, listen, did you ever talk to Richard and kind of drop it subtly that I was here?" And I told her I had talked to Richard.

Then she asked me if he had ever asked where she was living and if he had ever asked how he could get in touch with her.

I told her that he was very busy and that he said he was planning to call her but he didn't have time because he had had to go out of town. And she knew I was lying and she said, "What's his phone number?" I told her to ask information. She told me that I knew it wasn't listed, so I said, "Are you going to call him?" and she said, "Shouldn't I?" and finally I could say, "That's your problem, not mine."

She said, "Richard is the kind of person that doesn't like to commit himself and I think that he doesn't want to commit himself to me. I bet he's scared because he thinks that I came all the way out here just for him."

So I said, "Didn't you?" And she said, "I don't know. I don't know. I came out here partly for him, but really for me, too. I'm looking for myself. You know how they look in those letters to the lovelorn, for themselves? But I'm looking for myself somewhere under a desk or a table. You know, when I was in high school girls had to take Shop, and once one of the teachers who was teaching me how to make shelves dropped a nut or a bolt or a screw, I don't remember, and we started hunting for it under all the tables and the desks, and one of the kids said, 'Oh, look, Mr. Ferris is looking for his brain,' and everybody roared. Poor old Mr. Ferris felt like a jerk, because I guess he had been looking for his brain, and that's the way I feel. I'm looking for myself under a table."

She said, "Do you think I'm a phony?"

And I said, "No, I think you're a lemon."

And she said, "Not a peach?"

And I said, "Okay, Nellala, you're a peach."

I used to talk to my wife about Nellie. I told her how she came out to California all by herself, and how she let me put her to work at the coffee house, and how she was still trying for her big chance with her own bit, and how she was doing all those things just because one guy—a writer yet—was giving her a bad time. And my wife— who was usually jealous if I talked a lot about the clients when they were girls—wasn't jealous when I talked

112

about Nellie. One night my wife said, "Why don't we invite that kid over for dinner?" and that was funny because I said, "What kid?" and my wife said, "Nellie."

It was funny because it was my wife who thought of inviting Nellie, not me. It turned out to be very nice because everybody liked everybody else, and everybody had a nice time, especially Nellie. Later she told me how much she liked my home and how much she liked my kids, and she said she thought my wife was so nice and such a good mother, and she sighed, "Jewish parents sacrifice themselves, don't they?"

And I said, "Well, you don't exactly sacrifice. You just try to give them a chance to be better than you."

And she said she once heard that was the whole basis of the Jewish family—all the parents wanting all the children to be better than they were. But maybe that was the way they got into trouble—the parents *and* the children—because if the parents didn't think they were good enough for the children, how could the children think they were good enough for the parents?

So I told her that wasn't exactly the way it was, and it wasn't a question of good or better, it was a matter of doing the best you could. She thought and then she said, "I guess you're right. But don't you think Israel is a bit much?"

I told her that Israel was the Promised Land and we got what was coming to us.

And she said, "Everybody gets what's coming to them, don't they?"

One day the guy who ran the place where she was working called me. He said he wasn't calling to complain or anything, and you can imagine how that got me nervous, so I asked him if he wasn't calling me to complain what was he calling about. He said that Nellie was doing a very good job but that he didn't like the way she was drinking. Not that he begrudged her a drink—but after all it was a coffee house—and if the help was drinking the customers would want a drink and maybe they would get the idea to go somewhere else. And I asked him how she got the drink. And he said, "Look—it's not *a* drink, it's a lot of drinks. She keeps a bottle back in the dressing room. Nat, I don't want to get her in trouble or anything, but she could get me in trouble. Tell her to knock it off, okay?—Or else I'll have to get rid of her. . . ."

I told him not to worry and not to get rid of her, and I called her in and I asked her if things were okay over there at the club. She said, "Over at the Bloomsday Club?"

I said, "What are you talking about? It's not called the Bloomsday Club, it's called the Casa Gatta." And she said, "It is indeed called the Casa Gatta, Natto. Casa Gatta—do you know what that means?"

I said I thought it meant that it was like one of those places where you go and talk like in Italy.

She said, "Honestly! Amos Agent, the Ignoramus. In Italian, Casa Gatta means Cat House."

So I said, "That I didn't know. And let me tell you, if I knew. . . ."

She said, "If you knew you'd have booked me there anyway."

"Not necessarily."

"Not necessarily, Natto, but in all probability." She said, "You know, if I ever started a nightclub I wouldn't pull any punches. I'd call it the Black Pussy Cafe, like the one in W. C. Fields' *Bank Dick*. Or maybe I'd open a saloon where I was the lady bartender and singer, and then I'd call it McSorleys West and only allow men customers to enter. You know about the real McSorleys, the one in New York? I once went there dressed as a boy because they only allow men, and I got kicked out because they noticed my breasts."

I told her that till she opened her own club she should lay off the booze. She said, "My friend, the fink-manager-squealer, on top of everything else?" And when I said, "On top of what else?" she just laughed and said, "*That's* his problem. He wants to be on top of everything and *everybody* else, besides, before, behind, underneath and in front. Hah!"

I didn't like that kind of talk from her and I told her that it wasn't nice for her to use that kind of smart talk that she was picking up, because she'd smart-talk just like all the other girls. She said, "If you don't want me to smart-talk like all the others, and if you think I'm different, why don't you get me an audition or a test for something, so I can get out of there?"

I told her I was working on it, and I was. . . . But that I wasn't going to go around selling a boozer. And if she wanted to be sold on a high-class level she'd better act high-class, and just watch her step and make sure everything got straightened out over there at the Casa whatever.

She said, "You're ashamed, aren't you?"

I said, "I'm a little bit ashamed, Nellie, but you should be more ashamed."

And she could tell I wasn't kidding around, and she said, "Okay, I'll reform."

"Good."

"I'll stop smoking."

"Very funny."

Then she said, "I'm going to call Richard." I told her I thought she was going to call him before. And she said, "I was trying to be hard to get, but it didn't work."

Like I told my wife, she wasn't the kind that went around kidding herself.

She finally got Timon on the phone, and they started seeing each other. I don't know how he handled both of them—Nellie and the Italian—at the same time, but he played them off against each other and they both took it without bitching, except for one day when Nellie said, "I really wish that Richard would let me move in with him because that Italian is bad for his stomach. You know, he has a terrible stomach and he needs somebody like me to watch it."

I told her that a lot of people, including my wife, figured that Richard could take care of himself and his stomach as well as the next guy. And she said, "No—neither you nor she can understand. See, you've got Rose to take care of you and she's got you to take care of her. The truth is that nobody really can take care of themself all by themself. They've always got to have somebody to take care of them. Except for the strangelings. . . . See, it's not that I need anybody, but it's just that people always have to have somebody. See? It's like my having you. Ten percent of me is taken care of by you."

And then she said, "That's a lousy thing to say, isn't it? I mean, I know that you care about me more than ten percent, don't you?"

I told her I cared about her a hundred percent, and she said, "No. A hundred and ten percent. It's funny about percent, isn't it? On a scale from one to ten, I love you nine." And I asked her how much she loved Richard and she said, "I love him ten, but I think he only loves me six or seven. I mean, if you had me how could you want anybody else? That Italian, that foreigner, she's very destructive. In a lot of ways. I mean, she's destructive coming over here taking jobs away from Americans. . . ."

"Like you."

"Exactly like me. And she's very destructive to Richard

116

in other ways besides his stomach. He should just have me and then everything would be fine."

"For who?"

"For everybody. Including you because then I wouldn't bug you. Listen, come on and get me a job in the movies."

I told her that as a matter of fact there was a picture—maybe—over at Paramount where she could get a little job—maybe. And she thought that was "incredibly lovely" and what would she be? I told her she'd be the young girl and she said, "How pedestrian."

I told her not to count on the job but I'd see what I could do. She said, "*Arrivederci,* if you know what I mean," and off she went. I don't know to where.

I think she hung out with the kids on the Strip. That was probably where she picked up the stuff about the foreigners taking jobs away from unemployed Americans. I don't know if she had other boyfriends. Once she said she used all her spare time to work on her singing. I told her that was very nice and to keep busy.

She had to do something during the day besides sleep, or sit knocking her head against the wall waiting to hear from Timon. I bet she sat and waited until he was in the mood. I knew all about his tactics. His wife used to write to me when he didn't send her money. Some letters, let me tell you.

I'll bet that even though Nellie knew all about the Italian the Italian didn't know about Nellie, because that Italian wouldn't have taken it lying down. So Nellie and Timon probably had to make it at her place, and Nellie probably sat there waiting to hear from him. At least that's the way I figured it, and Rose agreed with me and she thought it was a shame, a nice girl sitting around waiting for a writer. . . . I said, "Better a writer than an actor." And Rose said, "But he's married! And she has

117

such lovely manners she could make someone a wonderful wife."

Nellie never drank when she came to the house, and she always talked about how sorry she was to have to give up her schooling, and Rose thought it was a shame that her parents didn't think enough of her to let her finish her education. So I told Rose she was an orphan. What else could I tell her?

Then one time we were invited to a party by Abe Shinestein, today's version of a tycoon. Today the big muck-a-mucks like to go back and act like they think Louis B. Mayer acted. Not that I'm saying anything against Abe Shinestein, or Louis B. Mayer, just that sometimes Abe Shinestein was a little old-fashioned. He was very much for clean, decent pictures. He said, "Dirty pictures make me want to vomit."

But, aside from that, he invited us to this party and Rose said we should take Nellie, so I said, "You call her. That's nice manners."

Rose called her and naturally she asked what she could wear and Rose said, "Something informal. It's a cookout on Sunday afternoon at the Shinesteins'," and according to Rose Nellie broke up and said, "I know his son Howard. I know him from Harvard." And Rose thought that was wonderful because if Howard was there Nellie could get into that younger crowd. I thought, "It should only be."

We picked Nellie up for the Shinesteins' and she was wearing one of those Jax dresses and she whispered, "I've got absolutely not a stitch underneath. How do you like it for ten percent?" And I said, "I'm probably liking it for a hundred percent. When do I get the bill?"

Howard Shinestein remembered Nellie all right. From Law School. When I heard Law School I almost fainted. Howard asked her why she had dropped out so fast and she said she found out she had to have an operation. One thing about Nellie, she always told the truth. He said he always thought she was married. And she said she didn't see what that had to do with having to have an operation. Again, I almost fainted. She told him that she had been married and that she wasn't any more, and how was he doing? He told her he had dropped out too, and she said, "You know what they say. 'Look at the man to the right of you and the man to the left of you, they won't be here next year'?" And they both laughed, and she said, "I wonder who was in the middle."

Later, when I asked her about Law School she said, "I only studied Criminal Law—but see how I met all kinds of people?"

Howard Shinestein took Nellie over to meet his father, and Nellie gave me a wink. Rose was in heaven. She could already see Nellie as Mrs. Howard Shinestein. I wasn't in heaven. I was in limbo. And I just watched the introduction.

Abe Shinestein may vomit from dirty pictures, but he likes girls like Nellie, and I could see he liked Nellie very much. And Nellie liked him and she liked his son Howard, and she liked Mrs. Shinestein and all the rest of the family. And Rose may have been thinking of Nellie for Howard, but I think old Mr. Shinestein thought of her for himself instead of for his son, and it was a little embarrassing for everybody. Only my Nellie could get into a situation like that.

She asked me if the picture that had the part of the young girl in it was a Shinestein picture and I told her no, but that there were other pictures that he was doing with other parts, and she said, "Oh, I don't want to make it that way. I want to be like the really big stars and just sleep with the hairdressers and the cameramen." Where she got those theories, I don't know.

119

Howard Shinestein started calling her from the very time he first saw her at the party and she told him she couldn't go out at night because she worked, and he told her he'd pick her up after work and she said she would be too tired. Too tired for Timon she wasn't, just too tired for Howard Shinestein.

Once she gave Howard a big break and let him take her swimming over at the house. That I would of liked to see. Her swimming, and the kid and the old man both looking. I once asked her how often the old man called her and she said, "You know he's very smart. He got the message right away. About his son and all. I mean, that kind of thing is disgusting. Even though I don't like Howard really—it's crossing generations and that's like inbreeding."

She strung Howard along like he was a bellhop. Once she said, "He thinks he looks so Brooks Brothers, but he really looks like a bellhop."

Go ask God why Nellie didn't play her cards right with the Shinesteins. Maybe just out of plain perversity. Perversity is a word that a lot of my writers use, and God, do I know what perversity means. Rose kept saying, "But she could have had such a wonderful life with Howard. He's a fine boy and nice-looking. What is it with her?"

Nellie got the "young girl" part in the Paramount picture and her only reaction was that the whole thing took too long—getting it and doing it. "It takes them three weeks to say 'Hello' much less 'Goodbye' out here." I told her the studio liked what she had done. And she said, "I was on good behavior—for you. And I knew they'd like me, so I quit my job."

"You quit your job?"

"Well—not yet—but now that I'm going to be in the movies I can't have the image of slinging around for a living in the Cat House."

"It's a coffee house, and pay back what you owe before you quit any jobs."

"I paid you back."

"How much do you owe Timon?"

"I don't owe him anything, and if you were smart you'd know it."

"So who else do you owe?"

"No one you would know."

"Where'd you get all the clothes?"

"I borrowed them."

Later on I found out she owed my wife a couple of hundred dollars. I didn't care about the money, it was the principle. I was Nellie's agent, so if she needed the extra money she should have asked me, not my wife.

I got her a couple of television jobs, mostly in the serious Westerns.

She said, "They hire me because it saves them buying a wig."

She was making nice money, and for a while there she was laying off the booze. She handled the whole thing of quitting her job by herself. She told me she spoke to her friend, the fink-manager who liked to be on top, and told him she wanted to take a leave of absence for a while, so that if things got bad for her she could come back and be announced as coming back by "popular demand." She gave the guitar to one of the girls in her building, and when I gave her a look she said, "Don't worry, star-maker —just on loan."

I started getting calls asking who she was and what she could do, and I started taking her on rounds. I told her it was classier when the agent comes too, and she said, "Better than when the mother comes too. Remember the Jack Buchanan song?"

But I had no complaints. She wanted to work and she behaved herself very nicely. It was a pleasure to go around with her. She knew just which directors to play up to, and just which ones to play down to. She had dinner one night with Howard Shinestein and it got in a column. . . . "Eastern-society-girl-turned-show-biz dueting at LaScala with Howard Shinestein. Will he make the sun shine for Nellie?" She told me she planted it herself and I told her it sounded like it. But she knew that I knew it was good for whatever that kind of thing is good for.

Like I said, she was a pleasure. Usually, when you take a girl around it's like carrying a lox that doesn't know which end is up. Not Nellie. I told her she should have stuck with Criminal Law. She would have made it.

And she said, "I'm making it now. Richard had a fight with the Italian. Isn't that the end?"

"Did you move in with him?"

"Not yet. He thinks it would be bad for my image now that I'm doing so well. . . ."

"But it's you for him and him for you, right?"

"Right."

"And the Italian's being deported?"

"Back to Sicily."

"Don't count your chickens."

"Don't you want me to be happy?"

I told her that I wanted very much for her to be happy and that I could see she was going right on the road to not being happy, and that if Timon and Boston weren't enough to show how she wasn't going to be happy, just the fact that he waited so long to come around in California should have been enough. Enough yet, without the fact that he still wasn't divorced. And she got mad at me because she said, "Look, I'm coming through for you and I don't tell you how to live, so don't tell me."

I said, "I'm not telling you, I'm begging you. . . ."

And she said, "Well, take your cup to the next corner."

122

When I told Rose how she talked, Rose told me that I should practice what I preached and never tell anybody how to live their life. She told me that the worst thing you can say to a person is that the one they want is no good, and that no matter what happens or how bad the one they love turns out to be, the one they have it in for is the one that told them. And I needed Rose to tell me that like I needed Rose Franzblau, but I couldn't take it back. Could I? Like Rose would say, even when you take it back you still said it.

Rose said I should try to make it up with her, so I asked her if she wanted to bring Timon over for dinner. She said would Rose be mad at her. And I told her not to worry but to bring him, and that Rose was glad for her that she had what she wanted. At first she didn't believe me and then she said, "I guess Rose is smart. She knows you can't help loving who you love, and if you choose wrong—that's your problem. And you live with it."

So we set a night and they came over. He was in a good mood, and Nellie? Nellie was in heaven. It was like when he said, "Pass the salt," she wanted to get up and applaud. She would pass the salt like she was passing the Crown Jewels, and he would act like he was getting them.

Except for having to sit through that, we all had a nice time that night, and then after dinner I told Nellie that I might have something good for her. They both wanted to know what, and I told them that I had met a guy I knew from New York who was rich and had some money he wanted to put into a new restaurant. He wanted to make it a New York type of supper club for all the people from the East who have to come to California to work. They both thought it was a great idea, and Timon said that it would be like the *New York Times* franchise, and Nellie told him that nowadays the *Tribune* was "in," and he said, "In with the ones that like big print," and they both thought it was very witty. I thought as brilliant as "pass the salt."

Nellie wanted to know all about the guy and the restaurant, and I told her that the guy told me he wanted to make it like Gatsby's or Goldie's in New York, so I told him about her "twenties" singing bit and he thought she sounded like the kind of act that would fit in. And she got up from the table and she hugged me, and she said, "Oh God, if you get me this job I'll marry Howard Shinestein so I can get jobs for all your clients," and Rose said, "Don't worry about the jobs, just marry Howard Shinestein," and we all laughed. But I could see Timon was laughing out of the wrong side of his mouth.

Everything was like they say, "hunky-dory," and then one night it all blew up.

It was maybe four, five o'clock in the morning, and Rose and I were sleeping, then Rose woke up when she heard the front doorbell ringing. She was scared. From a little beginning, the bell started ringing and ringing and ringing. We started to get up and we heard the pounding on the door and at the same time the bell kept ringing, and the kids heard it too—like, how could they help it? And they started screaming because they were scared, and they started yelling, "What's happening?" And they screamed, and we heard the ringing and the pounding and screaming from downstairs, from the maids, and outside.

Rose ran in to the kids and I ran down the stairs, and it all seemed like it was taking a long time, but it wasn't. It was like they say what happens in a fire when you move so fast and it seems so slow. I got to the front door just in time to see Nellie—all wild-looking with her hair like a crazy person and her clothes half torn off—I saw her put her fist through the window. I don't know. . . . She was half laughing, half crying. . . . And upstairs they were crying, and Nellie was trying to push in through the broken window so I ran outside and she went for me—like with "Why didn't you let me in?" and with dirty language, and I started taking her inside and the blood was all over me and all over her, and then she said, "My mother killed herself. The dirty bitch! She killed herself, and then I went to Richard's and that wop was in bed with him and they were making it and there was nobody that wanted me, and I don't care. And I'll fuck them all and they'll be sorry. . . ."

And then Rose came running down and tried to grab a-hold of her and she took her into the downstairs bathroom and she tried to wash her, and Nellie kept hitting Rose and pushing her away, and she kept up the screaming, the screaming, "I want my mother, I want my mother, I want my mother, and nobody wants me!"

And she kept trying to beat herself on her belly, and on her arms where she cut herself, and Rose and I held her down and we poured some liquor down her throat, and finally she just went into a crying jag. She stank from liquor and blood and dirt and God knows what else, and Rose got her down into a chair and she started washing her and she told me to call a doctor, and when Nellie heard that she got up again like a crazy person and she started hollering, "No no, don't call a doctor! It'll be in the papers and they'll all say I'm no good," and then she came at me and she started hugging me and kissing me and telling me she'd do anything I wanted. The kids were watching. It was disgusting. And it was terrible. Finally she stopped and she hung her head down and she said, "Please don't hit me," and she passed out.

We washed her off and we looked at the cuts from the glass and they were what you would call minor cuts, so we decided not to call a doctor because who needed the whole thing. And it wasn't like it was an attempted suicide, it was that she was just trying to get in the house, and the stuff about the suicide of the mother we didn't understand, but we figured she'd tell us. We figured she'd been lonesome, so she thought she'd surprise Timon, and it turned out that she really did—so she must have been drunk and when she saw what she saw and what she didn't want to see, she flipped a little. We knew that a doctor wouldn't help.

We put the kids back to sleep and when they asked we told them that someone had tried to rob Nellie and that's why she was so scared and came running to us.

We put Nellie to sleep in the guest room, and then we had coffee and we stared at each other. "Go try to be nice to someone and this is what it gets you."

Rose said, "Should we call Timon?"

I said, "In the morning."

And Rose went back to sleep in the kids' room and I sat up because I would have been up anyway, and at eight o'clock nobody else was up so I went in to the office.

Rose tells it that Nellie woke up about three o'clock in the afternoon and she came downstairs and told Rose she was very sorry if she had caused any trouble. And Rose gave her a cup of coffee and told her it was perfectly okay, but not to make a habit of it. Nellie looked at the cuts on her arm and she just said, "Nice girls shouldn't play with broken glass," and Rose said, "Nellie, Nellie, we want to help you. I mean about your mother."

And Nellie said, "What mother?"

Rose said, "Nellie, you can talk to me?"

And Nellie said, "Girl talk? Okay—girls will be girls."

"Did somebody call you and tell you your mother killed herself?"

Nellie said, "My mother killed herself years ago."

126

Rose asked her if she wanted to go home for a while, and she said, "Home to where?"

So Rose didn't say anything.

And neither did Nellie.

Then the kids came into the kitchen and Nellie made with them like she always did, and they backed away from her, and Rose explained how they had been a little upset.

So Nellie asked Rose if she could borrow some clothes. Rose gave her a skirt and a blouse and she went upstairs and got dressed and came back down and borrowed five dollars and said, "Thanks for a terrific evening," and she walked out.

Rose called me and she said, "Listen, Nellie just walked out of the house and I don't know what to do," and I said, "Don't do anything. Relax." And she said, "How am I going to relax when a *mashugenna* comes screaming at my door at five o'clock in the morning and bleeds on my carpet and then walks out with her nice manners and says, 'Thank you very much?'"

I told Rose to take a Librium—she can't take Miltown —and she said that I should take a Librium and that she would take care of herself, and she hung up on me.

Then she called back twenty minutes later and she said, "Timon's here, what should I do with him?" I told her to put him on the phone.

I've got to say one thing about Timon. He had a great sense of self-preservation. Nine o'clock in the morning I called to tell what was going on and what happened. I told him how Nellie told us about catching him in bed with the Italian. I told him how she said she just found out her mother killed herself. I told him she put her hand through a window. He told me not to worry, that he'd take care of everything.

His way of taking care of everything was showing up at my house at four o'clock when everything was over.

Rose put him on the phone and he said, "Where's Nellie?" He said, "Where's Nellie?" like I was hiding her out.

So I just said, "I don't know. Maybe she's up at your house." And he said, very seriously, "No, I just left there." And I said, "You're a real Flash Gordon. You move to the rescue with the speed of light."

And he said, "Quit kidding around." I swear that's what he said. But he was my client, so all I said was, "Listen, Timon, all I want to know who is kidding who in this whole mess?"

So he said, "Do you really want to know?" and I told him that I really wanted to know because I didn't like finding myself in the middle.

So he said if I wanted he'd come right over to the office and we'd have a drink. That was very big of him.

I told Elsie, the receptionist, to keep trying Nellie's number and that if she still didn't answer to try to get one of the other girls in the building, and for all I know I must have blown a couple of deals that day because the way I felt and the way I was, I couldn't think, and when Timon came over we sat down with a drink, and he leaned back and he said, "Okay, this is the bit. The bit is that she's a flip."

Big news.

I told him I didn't think she was exactly run-of-the-mill, and he said, "You don't get it. She's really crazy." He said, "Not you nor me, nor anybody'll ever get a straight story on her. I've tried and I know." When I asked him how hard he tried, not to get a straight story, but how hard he tried in general, for once he didn't laugh.

And I didn't laugh either, because when you get into a situation like this where there's a kid involved who screams about her mother killing herself and who breaks

128

windows and who tries to beat herself up where she's bleeding—I can't tell you what it was like because it was like nothing I ever saw, and God willing, should never see again—when you get into a situation like this you have to call a spade a spade, for your own sake as well as everybody else's. And with me, I had my family to think about so I decided I would just ask Timon what was with him and Nellie and the Italian, and don't think I wasn't wondering whether or not he was making them play like in those foreign movies. I usually make it a big rule not to ask my clients about their sex lives, but this time, it was different, because the sex life was getting into my life. So I said, "All right, what's the story?" and he said, "Look, she wants everything. She's dependent, possessive, bitchy, but she's amusing," and I said, "Which one, Nellie or the Italian?" and he looked at me and said, "Both."

And I said, "Just tell me the part about Nellie," and he said, "First off, she wants to get married," and I said, "Doesn't everybody? It's like having an abortion . . . that's a quote, son, from Nellie."

He said, "Listen, you know I'm married. I know I'm married. You know I'm not divorced. I know I'm not divorced. Simple. . . . One, two, three . . . right? So Nellie should know too. Right? Wrong. Three, two, one—whooooosh—you're a malted—because facts don't count with Nellie. You get a divorce and you get married again —and you marry Nellie?" He was talking the truth. He said, "The Italian *doesn't* want to get married to me or to anyone that's not a millionaire. Sometimes I think she's holding out for the Pope. But it's fine with me. And if she's a little jealous, well, it fits in." And I said, "With what?"

"With the way an Italian should be."

So I tried to find out from him why he kept seeing Nellie even though the Italian was jealous and he said, "I get a kick out of it." And I said, "What? The Italian being jealous or seeing Nellie?" and he said, "Seeing Nellie" and I said, "If you don't watch out you're going to get a kick in the ass."

And he said, "You know, she's an alcoholic," and I said, "The Italian?" and he said, "No. Nellie."

He told me that Nellie was a secret drinker. And I told him that it wasn't such a secret that she was a drinker. I told him how they knew she was drinking at the club and how they told me, and how she knew that I knew, and I told him that I'd seen her drink in public so what kind of secret drinker could she be? And he explained to me that secret drinkers always drink in public but in private they always arrange to have extra ammunition. They keep a bottle in the pocketbook or in a drawer or in the hamper in the bathroom. . . .

And I said, "Or in the dressing room? Look, she drinks in secret when she can't drink in public."

And he said, "What about when she takes the drink before the drink? Didn't you ever smell it?"

I told him that I smelled vodka on her breath. And he said, "Breath? With secret drinkers it doesn't smell on their breath. It smells from their pores. They stink from alcohol. . . . They reek. . . ." He told me about how Sophie Treadwell once told him that she knew a man who was blind but could tell if a person was a drinker just from the way their body stank when they walked into a room. I asked him if Sophie Treadwell was a girl I should know about and he said, "Yes, you should know about her."

I said, "Where does she fit in?"

He said, "She's a writer. She wrote *Machinal*."

I told him I didn't see it and he said, "It was a big grosser, but forget it."

Then we got back to Nellie, and he explained that

130

whatever he felt for her, he couldn't afford her. What he needed was the Italian who was a nice, uncomplicated, real woman who you could take on and take off like a pair of pants.

I told him I thought that was a pretty good way of describing their relationship.

But he went right on. He said that taking on Nellie would be a whole other story. He said, "She's got a system, you see. She gives so much that she figures you've got to give her something back in return. And she figures it right."

And he said that's why he was staying out of it. He said that I should stay out of it too, because there was going to be trouble sooner or later, and I said, "I can't stay out of it because there's not going to *be* trouble. Trouble is here and I'm in it, and I don't know about giving and getting something in return, but I know I've got ten percent of Nellie, and besides, I like her and so does Rose. She's a person."

And he asked me, "Since when are agents human?"

And I told him that they're human when they see a kid trying to put her hand through a window. He didn't answer. So I explained that I didn't think she was purposely trying to kill herself last night in particular but that she was trying to kill herself in general, and he said, "So what do you want to do? Let her kill you, let her kill me? She could do it. . . ."

He said, "I can't take her on because I'd have to take her on a hundred percent, and I'm not in any position to take anybody on one hundred percent—even myself."

So I brought it up that she had come all the way from the East Coast just for him, that she had the abortion and that she never even bothered him about it, and he said, "I know, and I don't forget and I see her and I give her what I can, but I'm not Mr. Middle Class and I don't want a house with a flowering vine, and how do I know it was my baby anyway?"

He said, "You don't understand. Nellie lives by and according to her own rules. She thinks she can go as far out as she wants to go and do everything she wants to do. She thinks she can walk on trestles and not fall off, and lay down in the gutter and play dead and then tell a cop she's looking for a nickel she dropped. And she thinks you should lay in bed all day and screw and not work if she's working nights, and that you should get all dressed up and play and screw all night if she's working days. She thinks you should have pumpkin pie and vanilla ice cream for breakfast because it's a good combination, and that you should do everything you ever wanted to do, and then one fine day you should get married and suddenly become Ma and Pa Kettle. She doesn't understand that marriage *doesn't* make it straight! It makes it worse."

I told him he had a very nice marriage to prove that point.

He said, "I'm telling you here and now, I'm not accepting the responsibility. I'm not making Nellie my charity."

I told him nobody was asking him to make anybody his charity, only that he should do what was right. And he said, "Get off my back and mind your own business."

I told him Nellie was my business and so was he, so he said, "Then collect your ten percent and butt out." And before he got to the door I hollered to him, "Timon, she doesn't need charity. You do."

But he kept right on going.

And I felt bad, because even though he had a big mouth, I could see that he was feeling something. God knows what—but something.

There I was with a good client who had just told me in very plain language to mind my own business, and with

Nellie, who probably wasn't going to be able to be working for a while, and maybe never.

So I phoned Timon and I apologized—I crawled—and I told him as far as I was concerned, I'd never bring up the subject of Nellie again. I told him that I was the kind of guy that believes certain things are off limits and that he was right, and he could be rest assured that I was butting out of the whole Nellie thing.

And, God help me, I meant it. Because I knew I had a winner with Timon . . . and, God forgive me, I knew Nellie was a loser.

That night I went home and Rose asked me if Timon knew anything or if I heard anything, so what did I do? I did what you do when you're feeling that you've gotten it all day from everybody, including yourself, and you feel like now *you're* entitled to give it to somebody. So I gave it to Rose.

I told her the whole goddamn thing was her fault because she was the one who let Nellie run out of the house and because she was the one who started inviting her over in the first place, and I said that when Nellie walked out she should have tried to catch her, and Rose said she tried but Nellie had a cab waiting.

I told her that was a stupid answer, because how could Nellie pay a cab, and that was when Rose told me about how she gave her the five dollars, and that was when it all came out about how she had been giving her tens and twenties and God knows how much more, and that was when I let Rose have it, like I wanted myself to have it.

Rose cried and said she did only what any person would do, and I said, "Only what any dummy would do."

And let me tell you, I went upstairs and I cried too. I cried for all of us. But mostly because that kind of aggravation I didn't need.

For a week or two we kept calling Nellie's apartment house. She never answered. She was never there. One time we even called Howard Shinestein. He didn't know anything.

Then a girl called us. The girl she loaned the guitar to. The girl said, "Nellie asked me to tell you she was leaving town and that you'd hear from her. She said to say 'Thank you very much.' And she told me that I should come in to see you because you could get me a job."

So what do I do? I said, "Come in and see me," because I owed Nellie.

Why did I think I owed Nellie? Maybe that I made her play it my way and not her way. You tell me.

Anyway, she was gone, and what was I going to do about it? Nothing. She said I would hear from her, so I decided I would wait to hear from her, and I didn't say anything to Rose except that she left. Rose didn't even ask where? She didn't ask where or why and she was smart, because she knew Nellie was trouble between her and me. And that's the way we left it. And if we left it, as Nellie would say, like "finks," it was because we had our own lives to live. Doesn't everybody?

The Actor

I can say quite unashamedly that I am endowed neither with noble brow nor jutting jaw.

However, in all modesty I must admit the possession of finely chiseled nose and excellent cheekbones. Bones, you know, are the key to the actor's success—both on the boards and in the boudoir.

I am a Star.

A very big Star.

But I am an Actor, as well.

I am the beloved of the literati who deign to condescend to acknowledge that the drama, when properly executed, is a form of art.

I am also and as well a bull moose at the Box Office.

You see, on occasion I deign . . . I deign to lease my talent to the stinkpots and flesh peddlers of what is known as the Film—thereby becoming the Darling of the Delinquents.

I think I have a very nice life.

A nice life indeed. . . .

You there—you in the mirror—half shaven and half not—leave me alone.

How can I? You're always looking in the mirror.

A nice life.

Then why do you have to talk to yourself out loud?

Look! I stand as a giant Colossus striding two worlds . . . stretched between intellect and idiocy. . . .

You're half in heaven, half in hell. . . . Don't you ever wonder how you became what you've become. . . .

I loved Nellie. . . .

She made you what you are today—I hope you're satisfied.

I'm satisfied.

Do you ever think of Nellie?

I think of her all the time.

Brady, you're a fraud. . . . A Freudian Fraud. You're Galatea in Drag.

Does that make Nellie my Pygmalion?

Not quite. . . . Nellie was Nellie. . . .

And Nellie was Juliet and Rosalind and Lady Macbeth and Isadora Duncan and just a little bit of Helen Morgan and Ruth Etting and more Lady Brett Ashley and someone from Greece she called Aspasia, and I called her Baltimore because of a disc jockey whom she could never find, and because you had to go through Baltimore to get to Washington, which is the Center of Power.

When they told me she was dead I remember thinking . . . only the good die young because they're too good to live in this world. They can't take it, so they pull a Starr Faithful.

Starr Faithful was Gloria Wandrous in *Butterfield*

8. If you saw the movie, put it behind you. Read the book.

Nellie was born out of time and out of place and way, way out of joint. She was all for banning the bomb because she felt the H-bomb was the same thing as the bow and arrow only more so. She felt that if all the world were set out to kill her sooner or later, she'd fool the world and do it sooner. . . .

Not to spite the world, but despite the world. . . .

She was my wife.

She married me out of the goodness of her heart.

She married me in sickness, not in health.

She married me not out of love, but in spite of it.

She married me because she said that she thought that marriage takes care of loneliness and longing.

She married me on the straight and narrow, and I thought we both really meant "Until Death do us part."

Death didn't part us.

We were parted long before.

And now I feel like a character from Edgar Allan Poe. Now, at last, I possess her. I possess her in death, and I shall possess Sweet Nell forever.

"I have been unconscionably long in dying," said Charles II on his deathbed. "Take care of Sweet Nell." I used to lie on the bed and say that—and she'd laugh and say, "Thanks for the flowers."

> *"Hey, Nell. . . . Hey?*
> *Don't you remember?*
> *I was always your clown,*
> *So why try to change me now?"*

She died Mrs. Brady, remember?

• • •

I met her first time back in New York when I was wading through an off-Broadway dramatization of the Collected Works of James Joyce. Nowadays, it would be played off-off-Broadway. Very artistic. No audience . . . except for Nellie who felt Joyce not only demanded but deserved attention. She used to come down to the Village looking for singing jobs. She would go around telling all the people she met that she had been a professional singer in St. Louis. Everyone believed her.

Everyone but me. I told her she was full of bull. So she told me all about her Sound and Fury. She told me all about getting kicked out of school, and not caring, and posing naked for a middle-aged painter because she wanted to sing.

I wrote a poem for her. She loved the poem, but not me.

"Dear Nell. . . ."

She would appear and disappear. I used to say that she was the "Ghost That Walked." Everything I used to say means something else now.

Once in New York, she appeared at my door and stayed for six, eight days. Then she went back to her middle-aged painter.

And then she stopped appearing and disappearing altogether. I would think of her all the time. There's a Frank Sinatra record she always played on the record player. . . .

> *"Wait till you see her*
> *See how she looks*
> *Wait till you hear her laugh.*
> *Painters of paintings*
> *Writers of books*
> *Never could tell the half. . . ."*

138

Painters of paintings, writers of books. . . . That's the thing that kills me.

I was the husband.

Okay, the second husband.

To go back to the beginning, the James Joyce thing flopped and there I was with nothing. But I got a reading for a television pilot, and they flew me out to the Coast. The script wasn't bad, not really bad. But the director didn't know what he was doing. And like most pilots, it never sold, so there I was on the beach—or, to put it accurately, there I was poolside. There I was, and I learned that when you fail in New York you can say you've accomplished something, but when you fail in L.A., *nada*. I had nothing to do, nowhere to go, no money. . . .

One night I met a fugitive from my pilot, and he said, "Let's go down to the Casa Gatta," and I walked in and there was Nellie. I didn't make the first move. I just waited till she came around to our table, and looked, and she opened her arms wide and said, "Welcome to the Bloomsday Club, you old Daedalus, you."

We broke up laughing, Nellie and me, and started explaining the Joyce connection to my fugitive companion. I let Nellie talk . . . she always told things better than I. Then, after she finished, she let me take her home and we asked each other about both coming to the Coast, and we asked each other about how things had been in New York, and I asked her what happened when she disappeared and she told me she had gotten this great job in Boston that hadn't been so great, and she told me she had met a great man that turned out after all not to be so great. But she said she had come out here with him anyway and that then they had had a fight. A terrible, violent final fight. And now she was really concentrating on her career.

Sweet Nell. . . .

I knew she was lying. I could always tell with Nellie.

I had a lying-timer that went "ding" in the back of my head. I explained to her I could always tell when she was lying. She said that it meant I really loved her.

I loved her, I really did.

I used to haunt the Bloomsday Club and listen to her sing and play the guitar. She hated that guitar and that kind of singing. But she was good. I told her she was better at the guitar and that kind of singing than the kind of singing she referred to as "her act." Nellie said that was because I didn't have any taste and that anyone worth their salt knew the singing in the act—the real singing— was better.

She used to play the guitar and sing,

> *"Weep a tear for John Brady*
> *Seven long years he loved a Lady*
> *He was a simple guy*
> *Who meant it . . .*
> *When he said, I'll love you till I die."*

John Brady. John Brady, Jr.

When I changed my name, that's the name Nellie picked for me. I said, "Why John Brady, Jr.?"

She said, "Because who knows? Someday you may go into politics." At that time we thought it was a joke. It was pre-George Murphy and Ronald Reagan. She said, "You mustn't take one of those phony names like Eric or Christopher or Terrence. But—John and Brady sound successful and distinguished and honest, like John and Gilbert or John and Wayne. And the Junior makes it sound like you come from a family of actors. And anyway, think of the song and it'll give you a sense of what you should project. You know. The soulful lover type who really falls when he falls. Think John Brady and you'll be a star."

"Not six foot under where it's shady?"

"Never. You'll be a star and you'll be buried at Forest Lawn."

"Thank you, Nellie."

So I'm John Brady, Jr., the Star, and it's Nellie who's six foot under where it's shady.

People are going around giving me that "Do you think it was because of him?" look.

Nat Gench says, "Let them think what they think, you know what you feel."

Of course, Nat Gench—my agent—has a very good image of me.

He took me on because of Nellie. She used to say, "Nat Gench really rises above his name. And he's not just an agent, he's a true human being. Believe me, dollink." But that was afterwards.

Before I became a star I used to go down to the Bloomsday Club every night and sit and stare and listen till she finished all the sessions, and some nights she'd go out with me and some nights she wouldn't.

I knew all about the Writer. It was obvious. She never knew I knew, or that anyone else knew, but everybody knew.

And that's the part everybody forgets.

On the nights that we'd go out together, she'd always be a little nervous, as if she were missing a phone call. Everyone sensed it. Everyone knew Nellie was hooked on the Writer. They all knew I was a filler.

But I took what I could get.

And we had fun.

Once she asked me why I was an actor. And I answered, "Isn't everybody?" And she said, "Make love to me. And we'll pretend we're back in New York and you've just taken off your makeup and I'm still looking for a job . . . and I've come to the theater. . . . Hey! I said make love don't hurt me.

Nellie hated California. She told me the thing that killed her about California was that nothing was real. She said, "Do you know that joke about the two kids who are playing together, and one kid says to the other kid, 'We're poor. Our whole family is poor. My mother is poor, my father is poor, my brother is poor, my sister is poor, I'm poor, the maid is poor, the butler is poor, the chauffeur is poor. . . .' "

She said, "That's like California. They're crazy out here." And I said, "Why are you here?" And she said, "Because I'm crazy. Why are you here?" I said, "Because if I'm lucky, I'll get to do another pilot."

She asked me if I really believed I was a really and truly good actor. I said I believed it.

She said so did she—believe that I was a truly good actor, and that she didn't think I should try for a pilot but that I should go back to New York, even back to off-Broadway, and that sooner or later I'd be discovered like Geraldine Page and Jason Robards and George Scott and everybody.

She said you had to have Faith, like they did. "First you have to have Faith and then you'll be a Star."

But we stayed in California.

I stayed because I didn't have Faith and she stayed because of the Writer. People used to say he was very good. Nellie used to say he was better than good, he was awful. She used to tell me about him and Boston and about the abortion and about how he didn't believe it was his child no matter how many times she swore to him that it was.

She never understood how it killed me when she talked

about him. She never understood, or she never cared. She never knew that I knew that when she sang for me she was singing for him. She would sing, "Sweet and Low, Sweet and Low, Wind of the Western Sea," and "Oh, The Apple Trees," and "Avalon" and she would look way off over my shoulder and over my head. She once said to me that it wasn't fair, that some people didn't pay their dues, because she had to pay all of hers. She said, "Everybody has to pay their dues, don't they?"

I told her I didn't know.

She said, "Well, actors wouldn't know things like that. They're not in the club."

I was out of the club with two strikes against me, just because I was an actor.

Then she became an actress.

I asked her if that put her out of the club too, and she said she wasn't really acting, she was working, mostly because Nat Gench wanted her to. She told me all about Howard Shinestein and how she was starting to be an "insider" and how funny it all was, and then she quit the Bloomsday Club and I called her at her apartment, but she was always busy. I didn't see her for maybe nine— ten weeks. You always count by weeks in California, because of the unemployment insurance.

Then one rainy afternoon she showed up at my house. I had a little house in Laurel Canyon.

She had cuts on her arms and a bruised lip. I figured she'd been in a fight. She asked me what I was doing. I told her nothing much, sitting in the sun. . . .

She asked if she could have a drink.

I said sure.

She said,

> "Pussy said to the Owl,
> 'You elegant fowl,

How charmingly sweet you are,
Too long we have tarried,
Oh, let us be married. . . .'"

And she raised the glass as if to toast herself and drank the drink.

I asked her what the act was.

And she said, "Please marry me."

"For real?"

"For half real."

Then she asked if she could take a bath.

I said sure.

She said for me to come and talk to her while she took a bath. So I put the lid down on the john and sat there and watched her wash herself. She washed her own body like a mother might wash a child's. Very carefully. Methodically. First the right foot, and in between the toes, and then up the legs and up the body and then the right arm and then the face, and then the left shoulder and the left arm, and the left side all the way down to the left toes. She made me do her back and then she took the wash cloth and gave extra attention to the neck and behind the ears. Then gently, gently, washed her breasts and her belly. I told her that for all she hated the Japs she had a lot in common with them, and she asked me what I meant so I told her. "Water torture, don't you get it?" And she laughed.

Just when she was doing her neck she said, "So when shall we be married?"

I asked her what was in it for me.

She said, "I'll be a good wife. I'll read 'Dear Abby' every day and 'Making Marriage Work' and all those columns my mother used to read and that Italians read. Don't you hate them? Not the columns, the Italians? I don't mean prejudice-wise, and I don't mean the old-timey Italians, the real ones, like Dante, I mean the awful modern ones. Holy Mother of God—all the gangsters in the Cosa Nostra are Italian. I think you've even got to be Italian to get in. And all the trouble with the gangs and drugs and prostitution and everything comes from them —the Italians."

I asked her what the Italians had to do with our getting married. She said, *"Come si dice* 'vomit' *in Italiano?"*

Then she said, "You know, I hated my mother. It's only natural. I mean, I loved her but she was too beautiful, so I was jealous and ended up hating her."

I asked her if her mother was Italian.

She said, "Of course she wasn't Italian. She was a PWAP. That means a Pure White American Protestant. Hand me the towel. . . ."

She dried herself off in the same order that she had washed herself. And then she wrapped the towel around her like a sarong and she walked out into the living room. She kept talking all the while.

"My beautiful mother was a bona fide Perfect Pure White American Protestant. But that's a lie too. Because, you see, I didn't have a mother. And I didn't have a father, and I didn't have a brother and I didn't have a sister, and I didn't have a maid and I didn't have a butler and I didn't have a chauffeur. But I've got you. Don't I?"

"You've got me."

"I've really got you, and I'm going to do good for you. I mean, I'm going to try my best to be everything I possibly can be for you, and you do want me, don't you?"

"I want you more than anything."

"And more than anybody?"

"More than anything or anybody."

"Show me. . . ."

I made love to her. And there we were, lying naked.

She said, "How come you can love me even though I'm a nobody?"

"I don't think you're a nobody."

"I'm the prototype nobody."

Then she said,

> *"I'm nobody. Who are you?*
> *Are you nobody, too?*
> *Then there's a pair of us."*

She said, "That's from Emily Dickinson and we're not really a pair because you're not a nobody. You're a somebody and I'm the Nobody. But we'll get married and pretend to be Mr. and Mrs. Middle Class, except that we really won't be. You see, I see you in color."

Then she told me about Helen of Troy and Paris and Menelaus. She said, "You see, there's a play *Tiger at the Gates* which has a much better title in French—in French it's *The Trojan War Will Not Take Place*. In that play Ulysses says to Helen of Troy, 'Helen—you've got to stop all this nonsense. You've got to give up Paris and go back to your husband.' The husband was Menelaus. And Helen says, 'No, Ulysses, I will *not* go back to Menelaus because I don't see him in color. And I do see Paris in color.' Do you know what I mean?"

I told her not exactly, and she said, "When you don't have to be an actor, you'll know."

And then she smiled as if to apologize for knocking me for wanting to act, and she said that she didn't see me in color for *herself*, she saw me in color for *myself*. I asked her how she could see me one way for herself and one way for myself, and she said, "Well—the color equipment must have gotten broken down—"

And I said, "Ready when you are, C.B.," and made love to her again.

• • •

146

We were married by a Justice of the Peace. Neither of us had a religion that we practiced. Nellie said that if she could believe she would want to practice Catholic or Jewish because you either go all the way with Jesus or not at all. She said that she hadn't quite decided on Jesus being the Christ, but she did believe in God, the Father. She believed that He was stuck up in the sky somewhere and she used to ask Him for favors. And when I asked what kind of favors, she said, "You know, trading favors. Like, I promise Him that I'll be good if He'll give me something—like a job or a dress or a husband. And now I have one—a husband. And that's going to be you, isn't it?"

That was me, Nellie's husband.

And she ran the show. From the moment we said "I do" to that pariah of a Justice of the Peace.

I don't know if you've ever been married by a Justice of the Peace, but it takes about two, three minutes, and afterwards you look at each other and you're married, and you think—or at least, I thought—"What should we do to celebrate?" I'm the kind that always opens doors for ladies and such, so I said, "My bride. Mrs. Nellie. Dear Nellie. What do you want to do for a honeymoon?" And she said, "I want to go to the hospital."

Bad start.

But I drove her to the Cedars of Lebanon and she pretended to have appendicitis and she was great. Lee Strasberg would have been very proud of her. Moment of Truth and all. She moaned and groaned and they signed her right into a private room and they let me come up with her, and she locked me in the closet and then told the nurse that I had gone back down to the lobby to wait for the outcome of the tests.

They did all kinds of blood tests and pushing and they finally said that the tests didn't show anything, but that if she was in such agony, she ought to stay until morning anyway, if she didn't mind terribly. They handled her with double-kid gloves because she had made sure to tell them that it was her wedding day.

She said she didn't mind staying too terribly because the pains were excruciating and could she please have some Demerol.

While the doctor thought it over the nurse told her they hadn't been able to page me in the lobby, and she told the nurse that I must have gone to the bathroom because the sight of blood made me ill and hospitals terrified me. There I was in the closet trying not to laugh and wanting to bust her in the mouth.

The nurse said a few terse words about what cowards men were and left. Then Nellie got out of bed and said, in that marvelous slow, funny imitation of the Kingfish from *Amos 'n' Andy* that she did, she said, "Okay Andy, wheh's duh booze?"

I said, "In your bag, where else?"

She said, "That's mine, where's yours?"

I said that now that we were married what was hers was mine and what was mine was hers, and that I'd get tomorrow's, and she said, "That sounds like 'who's on first.' "

She got the bottle out of her pocketbook and we shared a drink in a sanitary Lily cup.

She said, "You know, I always spend my honeymoon in the hospital."

I said, "How nice for you," and I didn't push it. I knew that the Writer she was hung up on had been in the hospital in Boston, and I knew all about how they had shacked up there, and frankly this honeymoon-in-the-hospital was one area I didn't want to go into.

We drank some more and that was when Nellie told me I had to change my name.

I asked her why.

She said she didn't want to be Mrs. Albert Baker. Albert Baker—that was me.

She said it sounded like an Air Force code signal. Able-Baker to Albert Baker. I said I liked my name.

She said it wouldn't do, especially now that I was going to be a Star. That's when she struck upon the John Brady, Jr., idea.

I didn't want to change my name. I told her that even though I didn't like Albert, I liked Albie. Nellie said that her name was Helen but everyone always called her Nellie and she hated Nellie just as much as she hated Helen. And then she laughed and said, "Christ! No matter what you say, everybody in their heart hates their own name. That's why it's so exciting, you getting a new one."

She lifted up the bottle as if to christen me and she told me all those reasons why John Brady, Junior, was a good name.

I acquiesced.

And then she smiled beautifully and said, "Holy Mother, that makes me Mrs. John Brady, Jr. I have miles of names now. I was Mrs. Albert Baker and now I'm Mrs. John Brady, Jr., and I used to be Mrs. Whatchamacallit."

"You used to be Mrs. Falkenheimer."

"Please. . . ."

"Please what?"

"Please say you'll be John Brady, Jr. Say it, and it'll be my wedding present."

"I'm John Brady, Jr."

"And do you attest that all you say is true?"

"All I say is true."

"Do you love me best of all the rest?"

"I love you best of all the rest."

"Well, then, act like you're on your honeymoon."

So I did.

It's amazing, the fantastic utilization one can make of that gimmick on a hospital bed.

I left her room early in the morning, maybe five—six o'clock, and I sat in the lobby while they cleaned it up, and I waited until ten or so, when she was checked out.

They should have sold tickets for the performance.

It was brilliant.

She played it like Bette Davis in *Dark Victory*.

"Dahling, isn't it marvelous that I'm not ill? We can go home now. And you've been so patient, waiting the night for me. Last night was our wedding day, but today will be our wedding night."

When I say that Nellie ran the show, I mean it.

And when she said she felt I should go back to New York and "go off-Broadway," she meant it.

She said, "That's my plan. It used to be my plan for you, now it's my plan for *Us. N'est-ce pas?*"

What do you answer to "*N'est-ce pas*"?

"*Ça va sans dire.*"

"*D'accord.*"

Neither of us had any money in the bank so Nellie's plan was for us to break both our leases, and sell all the junk we had both accumulated separately because it was California junk and worthless, and try to scrounge around and get enough cash to fly to New York.

She shouted, "*Run*—do not walk—*run* for your life. Kill California before it kills you! No, there's no you, *tu*, any more, it's just you, *vous*, and *tu et moi* no longer exist because we're *nous*. So *nu?* Let's get out of here, dollink."

I don't know what love is. I think I've felt it . . . and I feel it still. I don't know. I used to think I knew. I used to think it was simple, inevitable.

Then I became Nellie's husband. Subtly, Mr. Husband.

She did give color to life. Even the bad times took on an air, a style maybe of some crazy adventure.

Like leaving California.

We both scrounged around and sold what little we could. But it was nothing like what we needed for the plane fare. So Nellie decided that we should steal records and sell them. She said that she had once known a drug addict that had a foolproof plan for stealing records. And if drug addicts could do it, why shouldn't drunks?

I told her I didn't think we were drunks. I thought we drank a lot, but we weren't drunks.

"What's the dividing line?" she asked. "When do you find out if you're just a heavy drinker or a drunk?"

"I guess the day there's no booze in the house. . . ."

"And it's Sunday. . . ."

"And you flip?"

"Right," she said. "So I'm a drunk. Always have been, ya know? Anyway—back to the records. And a quick get-away."

The plan was simple. She would go into a record shop carrying a large tote bag. She would ask for a Vivaldi or a Monteverdi record. The kind of thing they never push in California. I would come in and collect a lot of big-selling records that I said I wanted to listen to in the listening booth. By the time they found the weird record she wanted to hear I would have left the listening booth, leaving all my records in there. Then she would go into my booth, put all my records into her bag. She would emerge, holding the one Vivaldi or the Monteverdi, pronounce in a ringing soprano that the arrangement was atrocious.

The gambit was based on her manner and style and charm. All the record salesmen were so happy to have a customer who loved music and was beautiful. It worked. We pulled it in three or four shops. Then we sold the

151

records to a discount house and made about two hundred and ten dollars.

Nellie said it was nothing to be ashamed of—just a cathartic, dramatically speaking.

All in all, we raised the money and we left California a couple of weeks after we were married. If we hadn't had to go through the Cedars of Lebanon we wouldn't have had to steal the records. I never bothered to bring that up.

We got our tickets to New York and pulled out the armrest between our seats, the one that separated us, and we pulled a blanket over us and held onto each other because we had done it. We were going back to New York and we were both scared. Scared of New York and scared of all the commitments we had made to ourselves and each other. We came back to a city that we didn't know, a city that didn't know us.

Nellie said, "Remember? They'll sell you for a hatpin, much less a hat?"

We checked into the Yorkshire Hotel on 112th Street and Broadway. Nellie chose it because she wanted to live up there because of Barnard. I asked her if she was still pretending she was in school, and what did her parents think about her leaving California? She said her parents didn't know anything about her going to California, much less leaving, and that all that stuff about having stayed in school was all lies, and that she was a free agent. A free agent except for me.

She wanted to live near Barnard because of the educational atmosphere. She said, "They're trying to make it the Acropolis of the modern world." And she wanted to be near her friend, the painter . . . the one who couldn't paint faces. She said, "You know, I always thought that he just couldn't do things like eyes and mouths and noses

. . . but now I wonder if maybe he just couldn't do me. . . ."

She said that a hotel was a smart move. No one would know where we were living and that we'd move out, maybe downtown to the Village, as soon as we got work. Real work.

Then she rented a television set. She said it wasn't an extravagance. It was a business expense.

We would watch television and then she would turn it off and say, "Now—you act it out for me," so I would act it out for her and she'd say, "You're eight gazillion times as good. Too good for television. You're the real McCoy."

I said, "No, I'm John Brady, Jr."

"Dear John. . . ."

"Dear Nell. . . ."

Life was sweet. We were poor and life was sweet because we had nothing but each other and the television set, and of course, the books.

Nellie loved books. She had a whole trunkful shipped back from California. Some girl in her apartment building did it for her. She used to read and read. And I always knew what she was reading because she was always acting as if she were of the period and the people that were in the book she was reading. When she was reading *Typee* and *Moby Dick* and *Pierre,* she rose at dawn and drank ale because she identified with the men on the ship. When she worked her way up to *The Confidence Man* she used to sit for hours and try on different make-ups and disguises. When she read *Chéri* she lay in bed and ate chocolates and put cream on her face. When she read *The Age of Innocence* she concentrated on good posture.

She didn't believe in real things, only in images, only in things she saw in color. I tell you this only because it was part of Nellie and part of why she killed herself.

Once she asked me if I had to choose between reading and eating, what would I choose? And I told her that I knew what she was getting at but that frankly I'd choose eating. And she said, "Then you're going to be a Star . . . a big, big Star."

I am now what is known in the trade as a Star.

Nellie was always very honest about the fact that she thought it was not a man's job—a real man's job—to be an actor. But she would qualify her own value judgment, and say, "But I guess you *have* to be an actor because of your father."

"My father?"

"Yes," she said, "your father was a great silent film star who was a failure like John Gilbert. . . . You know that Sid Caesar routine where he's an actor like John Gilbert and when he has to make his first talking picture he goes to the opening and everybody laughs at his voice, and he turns to the producer and says, 'I told you that my costume was wrong.' Well, your father was an actor like that."

I told her that my father wasn't an actor, he was a cop. And she said, "How can you say that? Your father wasn't an actor? You're John Brady, Jr., the son of the great John Brady."

"I'm the son of Albert Baker, the cop."

"Never say your father was a cop."

"Why?"

"Because of the joke—'What does your father do for a living? Nothing. He's a cop.' "

And then I asked her who her father was.

"My father? My real father was a butcher."

And then she looked at me with those enormous eyes and arched that perfect neck, and she said, "I never told that to anyone in the world before." And two tears, like

154

child's tears, rolled down her cheeks even though she wasn't crying.

I took her in my arms and I told her there was nothing to be ashamed of, or anything to keep secret, her father being a butcher.

But she had a come-back. She said, "Dope! He wasn't just a butcher. He was a black-market butcher. That was the awful part. He made a fortune in World War II. He was just a butcher, but we were rich. And even though I was very little, I knew that we weren't rich like the really rich people. And after the war, he kept making money because of the black-market money. So the stench of the black market was on him forever . . . at least I thought so. It was so awful. I mean, all those guys dying and us having filet mignon."

She must have been three or four when World War II was over, so I asked her if she had gotten all this patriotic information from her mother. She said, "I never got the time of day from my mother, thank you. But back to you, John Brady, Jr. You were brought up in one of the great mansions of Hollywood and then when the talkies came in you all went broke and you had to sell newspapers. . . ."

"That makes me about forty-five."

"You look marvelous for forty-five."

"Come on, Nell, why can't my father be a cop? And I be me?"

"Because you have to have an aura. . . . It's got to seem like the reason you're a serious actor, not an actor-actor, but a really serious actor, is to make up for the failure of John Brady, Sr."

I told her that there was no John Brady, Sr., and that no one would remember him.

She said that was good because everyone would feel guilty for not having remembered him.

She got a job singing. She went downtown to the Village and got a job working in that dinky nightclub she had worked in when she first came to New York. I remembered how two years before she had gotten the job and worked only one night because she had been frightened. I asked her how come she went back, and she said it was because they let her sing as she really wanted to sing and that she wasn't frightened any more. Nothing could ever scare her again because she had nothing to be scared about—because she was a bona fide married woman.

That fits in with her killing herself.

Then she made a list of places for me to go and people for me to see, rounds to make.

She had a fantastically lucky instinct about what thing was going to hit. She was like that peculiar kid, Bobby Fischer, the chess player, who didn't seem to know too much, but to feel things. And to always be right.

I was offered a part in a company that was just starting, a repertory off-Broadway company, and I didn't want the part because it was small, and Nellie asked me what the part was and I told her it was Diomedes in *Troilus and Cressida* and she said, "Grab it, and thank God for it. He's the only sexy one in the whole damn play."

I took Diomedes and then I got Moe in *Awake and Sing!* Moe—the one-legged hero.

Then they did a revival of *Streetcar* . . . and I guess that Nellie had asked God for a trade or a favor because I got the part of Kowalski, and what was good for Brando was good for me. I always wondered what Nellie traded God for *Streetcar*, because suddenly I was a discovery.

Nellie said, "It's just like the discovery of penicillin. One day you're mold and the next day you're penicillin."

156

I thanked her for the compliment.

We moved from 112th Street and Broadway, from sardines and salami sandwiches, to Central Park West in the Seventies.

Nellie said, "This is the 'in' place to be, right between Lee Strasberg and Stella Adler."

We moved in a bed and a card table and we sat there in eight rooms with no furniture. Nellie said furniture would be coming.

Then someone sent me a Broadway play.

Nellie read the play twice, and she said, "Hah! Take it! I told you that furniture would be coming."

"Should I take it?"

"I'll kill you if you don't."

"Maybe I won't get it."

"You'll get it."

"Did you fix it with God?"

"No, Mr. Brady, this time I fixed it with the Devil."

And she started buying furniture.

She bought Irish hunt tables like other people buy end tables. And she bought clocks. We had all kinds of clocks. We had ship clocks and wall clocks and a grandfather clock that she put in one of the bathrooms. They have very big bathrooms in those old buildings on Central Park West. When I tried to explain to her that you don't put clocks in the bathroom because the steam from the shower kills them, she said that it gave her a sense, when she took a shower, of timing herself like an egg.

She bought two rocking chairs and an enormous sofa that was stuffed with down, and we used to sink way down into that sofa and read the play back and forth to each other. I played my part and Nellie played everybody else's. We worked together on every one of my scenes, and Nellie said she didn't know how the play was going to do, but that I was going to do fine. I said the Credit Manager at Lord & Taylor's was probably wishing he was as confident as she. All that goddam furniture.

She quit her singing job after she came to the first run-through of the play. She said it was important that she be able to go out of town with me.

I agreed.

She called her club and she said she was a nurse calling for Mrs. Nellie Brady. She said Mrs. Brady had burned herself on a hot plate and had been taken to the hospital to be treated for third-degree burns. The guy she talked to told her he hoped Mrs. Brady was okay and was there anything that he could do? She told him there was nothing he could do, and that Mrs. Brady said that she would call them as soon as possible but probably wouldn't be able to come back to work until her scars healed.

When she got off the phone, I said, "You did a great job, Nursie, but who's going to buy that hot plate story?"

She told me that people always believed that she lived in places where you had to cook on hot plates, so people always believed her when she gave out with the hot plate story. She said that even though she knew the play was going to be a hit, if it wasn't she could always go back to work.

I asked her why our life had to be full of "ifs" and "even thoughs," and she told me it was a good question.

She stayed with me right through Philadelphia, Boston, and New Haven. She stuck with me through the good reviews and the bad.

Philadelphia was easy. They loved me in Philly. But opening night in Boston! Reviews.

Elliot Norton called me "puerile." Nellie said I wasn't puerile because if I were she never would have married me.

Then she said, "So be extra-not-puerile the second night."

New Haven was if-fy, if-fy and even-though-y. Nellie said, "When we got married they shouldn't have said, 'Do you take him for better or for worse?' They should have said, 'Do you take him for good reviews or bad?' And I would have said, 'For always and for aye.'"

"Would you have sworn to always and aye?"

"I would have sworn—"

"And. . . ."

"And crossed my fingers—for good luck, you know!"

We opened, and the producer gave a big party at the Rainbow Room afterward.

Everyone came: the show-business people, the society people who like to think they're friends of the show-business people, the backers, and the columnists. It was a New York gossip column party. We waited for the reviews. . . .

The show was golden, in the cards, good for two years. . . .

And Nellie was very beautiful. She wore a white lace dress and white clockwork stockings and her hair hung all the way down her back, and she wore that kind of makeup that looks like no makeup, and she sat with good posture in a corner and drank champagne.

I could never get over to her corner because people kept stopping me and saying they had to talk to me, and then there were the pictures that had to be taken and when I kept trying to get Nellie in, there wasn't any chance.

When it was all over we went home. She said that it was a lovely party. I told her I was worried that she hadn't thought so. She said, "It was a lovely party, but for you, not for me."

I told her it should have been for both of us.

She said, "No, it was as it should have been. But I kept feeling that I should have been Mrs. Star, and you know what I felt like? I felt like Mrs. Dormouse."

I said, "But you should have come around and I would have introduced you to everybody."

And she answered, "Why didn't you bring everybody around and introduce them to me?"

I said, "I'll love you until the man in the Big Black Hat comes to get me."

"Who's the man in the Big Black Hat?"

I told her He was Death.

Then she murdered me.

She said, "Darling, you really are going to be a Star. You're actually misquoting the *Doll's House*."

Put another nail in the coffin for me. . . .

But we were rich, and we were happy.

Nellie called the club and told them she wasn't going to be able to come back because her scars were incurable. I asked her why she told them that and she said it was because she felt guilty. She said, "They were really nice to me and they went to all that trouble of getting the piano player, and they let me do all my own songs and they listened. . . . It's funny, isn't it? I think you love me. I mean I know you do, but you hardly ever came down to listen when I was working."

"Come off it, Nellie, I was working too."

"You used to come every night—to the club in California."

"Because I wasn't working . . . and anyway, I never liked that New York club right from the start and I never liked the idea of your going backwards to a place where you wouldn't work just two years ago. . . ."

"I wasn't going backwards. I was going forwards to where I'm headed for. . . ."

"Riddles, baby . . . ?"

"Why is a raven like a writing desk?"

"I don't know, but you've got butter in your watch, Mrs. Brady."

"Thank you, Mr. Dormouse. God! You really are the eternal actor. Picking up the cues but never listening. Anyway, it's a dead issue. I quit and I've retired to be Mrs. John Brady, Jr. *Voilà!* Read about me in the funny papers."

"Very funny, Nellie."

"Not so terribly funny. After all, I gave up a career for you."

"I didn't notice anybody running down to catch your bit. . . ."

"You mean Frank Sinatra didn't show so the party was a flop?"

"Nellie! Fins. Okay?"

"Okay, fins. . . . Finis. Like they say in the foreign movies."

Our friends were the friends that all young married actor couples have—other actors and actresses and their husbands and wives, and what-have-you, writers, directors, dancers. We got a maid named Maude and we had dinner parties. Nellie supervised the cooking. We had cocktail parties and drop-in parties and we were invited back to all the right parties.

Nellie seemed to like all the people when they were there, but she had a special time in her life, reserved to herself. She used to go over and visit her middle-aged painter friend, Mike Isaacs, all the time. She said our friends were very nice but they weren't real people and that Isaacs was her own real friend.

I asked her if she was posing for another naked portrait. She didn't answer. I never wanted to meet Isaacs and he probably never wanted to meet me. And Nellie chose to leave it that way.

She decided to go back to school, not to Barnard but to General Studies at Columbia. That way she could go to class during the day, and also at night while I was working. I told her she could do whatever she wanted to.

And she did.

But once when I was leaving for the theater, she said, "I'll be backstage to pick you up afterwards. Be extra good."

I could see her in the fourth row, a little to the right, and I played to her all the way.

She was with Nat Gench.

She brought him backstage and we were properly introduced, the proper compliments were exchanged. And then we went out for supper at the Plaza.

Gench said he wanted to handle me.

Nellie said, "Just for the West Coast."

Nat Gench said, "So is there any other Coast?" Nellie gave me a look as if to say, "Don't mention the Seacoast of Bohemia, he won't get it. . . ."

Nellie said I didn't need an agent for the East Coast because we had a lawyer. Nat Gench started arguing. Nellie said, "Nat—I'm Nellie. Never you-know-what-a-you-know-whater."

Nat Gench gave her a dirty look and said, "Thanks for cleaning up the language." I felt as if they were sending me back to Korea.

But they finally came to an understanding, and Nat said that dealing with Nellie was living out a chapter of *Portia Faces Life* . . . and I, the pie, was properly divided between lawyer and agent, East Coast and West. Nellie went to bed with a lovely sigh that night. She said, "I really did so well for you with Nat. And you're going to love him."

I said, "Just let him love me. Dollink."

Four weeks and Nat came through with The Picture.

Nellie was smug, a fat cat.

I was ecstatic.

Nellie said, "Ask Nat for double the money."

I asked him.

And he asked me if I was crazy. Nellie said to tell him "Yes, I was crazy," and hang up.

I sweated for two days. On the third day Gench called back and said double the money was okay, and was my answer "yes"? I said, "Yes, the answer is 'Yes.'"

When Nellie came home I told her, and she smiled her fat-cat smile. She said, "You see, I told you you'd be a star. And now you really will be. A movie star. John Brady, Jr., son of the famous John Brady, Sr."

"He couldn't make it in the talkies, right?"

"Right."

She went into the bar and got a bottle of champagne and handed it to me. She said, "I'll get the ice."

We had champagne on the rocks, and we toasted each other.

Nellie said, "You see, John-o, it was just a matter of coming back to New York and doing things the right way, instead of ass-backwards."

"Cheers."

She said, "To California, right? Cheers, tears, and roses, roses, roses. Clink?"

"Clink."

Then she said, "I'm not going with you. . . . Sshshu-uuuuuush. Don't interrupt. I'm not going with you—be-cause—you don't need me any more. Sshhuuuuussh. You see, you'll be a Movie Star and I'd just be your wife."

"And that's not good enough?"

"You'll be unfaithful to me and I'll be miserable, and I'll be unfaithful to you to spite you and to spite myself and we wouldn't have anything to build up on or to hope for because we'd have it all. We'd have everything, and we'd have nothing to look forward to."

"What do you want, Nellie?"

"I don't know what I want but I know I don't want to go."

She said she didn't want to go because she hated California. It was cold and it was damp—and that's why the lady was a tramp. She said she didn't want to go because she hated new movies and new movie stars.

"I only like old movies. New movies aren't real movies to me, only the old ones. More champagne? And new movie stars aren't real to me, only the old ones. It's funny, I dig John Brady, Sr., much more than John Brady, Jr. But that's not true, in fact, it's a disgusting lie, because I do dig John Brady, Junior."

"Then why won't you come out with me?"

"Because for you it's two giant steps forward . . . and for me it would be two giant steps backwards. And besides, we'd be in the Natalie Wood crowd. . . ."

"We wouldn't have to be in any crowd."

"We'd have to be in the crowd . . . and Natalie Wood's not important anyway. I'm not going, really, because I didn't marry you for me, I married you for you."

I did love Nellie. She was the most important person in the world to me. She wasn't the child she pretended to be. She wasn't the child that people thought she was. She was a calculated and calculating woman with what she called "the eye of an Osprey." And nobody has to tell me that all the chips had fallen into all the right places because of her.

But I swear I was committed to her and to that marriage, and to the both of us making it all the way together, and I don't think she ever really was. . . .

I tried so hard to explain to her how much I loved her

and how much I wanted her, and that I wanted her as my wife, but she kept drinking that champagne, and finally she said, "No—it's done. It's a *fait accompli.*"

She said she was a phase that I had gone through, and I was a phase that she had gone through; and that we both had gone through.

Then she told me how I really didn't want her. Of course, it was she who really didn't want me. And nobody but me knows that.

So I did the only thing I could do. I went to California to make the picture. And for a while I lived a monastic life of self-pity and prayed that she would come to me. But after three or four weeks, when the rushes looked good and the director was calling me "Baby," I started going out.

I still didn't hear from Nellie and I went out some more, never with one girl, always with a lot of different girls.

I think it was Nellie's fault.

But I guess if I'd really wanted her as much as I said I wanted her, I wouldn't have gone in the first place.

Still and all it was Nellie that made me go. It was Nellie that set it up.

And now everybody says that I treated her the way guys like me always treat their first wives. Everybody says she gave me everything and got nothing in return.

That's not true.

I loved Nellie and if she had come along with me, I would have been happy to have her.

I don't understand why everybody says it's all my fault.

Just because I'm successful and enjoying it doesn't mean I'm the one who crucified her.

The Teacher

Nellie Patch was the proverbial thorn in my side.

She had been a student of mine at Barnard College.

One Nellie Patch had been assigned to my Freshman English Class.

Early in her Freshman Year she elected to become an English major. I was appointed—perhaps anointed might be a better word—her temporary advisor.

When at midterm her name came up during a conference concerning the academic accomplishments of the Freshmen, I found it necessary to suggest that I felt that one Nellie Patch was neither qualified nor eligible to remain in school.

She did no work.

She talked aloud in class.

She giggled and distracted the other students.

She flouted all sense and semblance of academic discipline.

She showed no evidence of being what we deem "solid college material."

Her defiance was exemplified by her Freshman English themes.

The first example was a theme that was to have been at least five hundred words. The First Example:

"Once upon a time there was a little girl named Nellie whose father was a millionaire and whose mother was an alcoholic. The little girl named Nellie wanted to be like all the other little girls; but, unfortunately for her, she couldn't be like all the other little girls—because she was different from all the other little girls. Want to know why? Tune in tomorrow, same time, same station."

Seventy words *in toto*.

The first wasn't exactly a love letter, merely an overture. I called her in for her first conference. Again, in search of a better word, one might say confrontation.

I had a very small office, but it did not seem absolutely necessary that her right thigh be pressed so close to mine.

I began the first conference by asking the young lady how dare she submit such a theme.

She said, "I thought you'd want to know all about me."

I said, "Miss Patch. . . ."

She interrupted me.

"My real name is Mrs. Falkenheimer."

"You are registered as Miss Helen Patch."

"But in reality I'm Mrs. Helen Patch Falkenheimer."

"You have submitted an unacceptable theme."

"That was so we could have a long conference."

"On what?"

"On the desk?"

167

She giggled. I was an Instructor and she was a Freshman and she didn't know what she was doing to me, and so help me God, I didn't know what I was doing at all. I have often wondered if I had had her expelled—maybe removed is the better word—from school to solve the problem of what to do about her, or with her, or without her.

I said, "Miss Patch!"

"Please call me Nellie."

"I prefer to call you Miss Patch."

"Does that mean I have to call you Mister Winston?"

"It does, Miss Patch."

"Well, then, Mister Winston—I wrote that theme because you looked to me as if you'd be someone that could really be a friend to me."

"I'm not here to be your friend. I'm here to be your teacher."

"Then teach me something, 'teach.'"

"I intend to, Miss Patch. I intend to teach you a sense of responsibility. I am going to give you a failing grade on this theme and I expect you to make it up by handing in a proper theme."

"You mean, Mister Winston, a Show and Tell theme? What shall I show you, Mister Winston, and what more can I tell you?"

"You can show me and tell me. . . ."

She cut me off. "Back home we always had to start off with the things we did last summer. How about, summer before last I got married, and bored and divorced."

"Miss Patch, you can show me and tell me what you gathered about the hour spent on James Baldwin's *Go Tell It on the Mountain*."

"I didn't pay any attention to *Go Tell It on the Mountain*. I was gathering wool."

"That's not very funny."

"It's a *double entendre*."

"Miss Patch, I've got your message, and it would please me greatly if you got mine."

"What's your message?"

"My message is that I think you're a very intelligent girl with a faulty appreciation of literature and a smattering of French, and I would be most pleased if you would do your work and let me do mine."

"Yes sir."

"The theme is due on Tuesday next."

"Yes sir."

She walked to the door and said, "Aren't you curious about me and my family?" I told her that I was more curious about her punctuality and demeanor in class, and her theme on *Go Tell It on the Mountain*.

She said, "Mister Winston, I'm really not trying to be fresh, I really just thought you'd be somebody that I could talk to, and when you read that story to us the other day—*not* the James Baldwin one, the story about the boy and girl at the college weekend, the story about how they're scared to be together—I felt in my heart that I'd really like to read all the books in the whole world and understand them. . . . I wanted to read all the books in the world before I died. And I wondered if you ever felt that way too. . . . You're so booky-looking, Mister Winston . . . in a handsome way, I mean. . . ."

How does one define the ineffable essence of Nellie?

She would give you all kinds of trouble and then, quite unexpectedly she'd touch you—in a way that was so totally honest it was embarrassing. She would touch upon your secret image of yourself, and make it seem a reality. She was irresistible.

But I was an Instructor. I had no time for someone who was irresistible, much less ineffable.

It's strange, this teaching at a girl's college. It's as if

you take it on asking for trouble, and when the trouble comes, you pretend you never knew it existed. You pretend your career was all you ever cared for, and that you had never had the fantasy of all the girls falling in love with you. You pretend that you never had the fantasy of deflowering the better part of the Freshman Class.

I was not totally responsible for Nellie's dismissal. There was the Geology teacher. He was equally responsible. I used to see him occasionally in the teacher's lounge.

He would say, "Patch never attends class."

"Never attends class?"

"Only sometimes. Infrequently at best, and she refuses to memorize the rocks."

"What's her excuse?"

"She says the rocks don't know her, so why should she get to know the rocks!"

At that point the young woman who taught French said, "And she thinks she knows everything."

I said—in an accent—"juust zwat doo you mean by every-sing?"

"She treats all the faculty like they were fools."

I said, "*As if* they were fools. . . ."

"Like, as if, what have you?"

"You have grammar. The grammar of the English language."

Nellie's second theme—her make-up theme—was as much off the straight and narrow as her first. Her second:

"Darling Mister Winston,
    If I have to call you Mister, I insist on calling you
Darling. By the way, do you call yourself Mister in-

170

stead of Doctor because of the fact that you haven't completed your thesis? Tut, tut, must hand things in, you know.

I hate James Baldwin, but if you wish, I will comment upon Oscar Wilde.

I'm reading him on the side.

Would you like to know which side?

I think it only fair and fitting that if one does not care to read the assigned reading and one does read the unassigned reading, one should be allowed to comment—in depth.

By the bye, I looked you up in the Catalogue. I say Catalogue, not Catalog, because I'm basically a Miniver Cheevy. I looked you up in the Catalogue and discovered to my delight that you had matriculated at—or in?—the University of Minnesota. Tra-lah-lah! My father lives in Minnesota. In fact, he lives in Minneapolis, Minnesota. He left Mama and me and St. Louis and married a lady from the Twin Cities. Would you rather hear about James Baldwin? Or about Oscar Wilde?

Or do you think that Papa married that woman from the Twin Cities just so he could go to all the baseball games? God! I hope they don't ever win the pennant. Much less the series. . . . Do you know everybody in the Hall of Fame? Baseball-wise? I liked Babe Ruth's locker the best. Doesn't everybody?

After my father married the lady from the Twin Cities, Mama began quietly and politely to drink herself to death with great verve.

Tant pis.

Rumor hath it, Mister Winston, that you're shacking-up with the Intermediate French teacher with the lousy-accent. Honestly Mister Winston, *In-*

termediate French, much less a lousy accent. As for Oscar Wilde, he can best be summed up with an analysis of his comments concerning tying a tie.

If you can guess which play that comes from, I'll give you a kiss.

I know what your comments will be. Terribly stern.

'Patch! Too much icing and not enough cake.' Darling Mister Winston, that's been the story of my life.

Love,
Nellie"

Next confrontation.
"Miss Patch!"
"Yes, Mister Winston?"
The telephone rang.
"Excuse me for a moment, Miss Patch."
"Certainly, sir."
It was the French teacher. The Intermediate French teacher with her lousy accent. I told her that I was in conference, and would call her back.
"Miss Patch?"
"Yes, Mister Winston."
"I think you ought to see the psychiatrist."
"Pourquoi?"
"Miss Patch!"
"Not Nellie?"
"I am here to teach English Literature and Composition, not to be a counselor."
"Not even academically?"
"Academically, yes. Psychologically, no."
She began to walk about the room. It was such a small room and still she seemed to walk, never blocked, never stopping.

172

She told me that I was a true New Yorker, and that she had read all about them in the newspapers. She knew all about their penchant for watching people being stabbed and doing nothing except posing for the *Daily News*. Always after the fact.

"Miss Patch, you don't understand what I'm talking about."

"Unfortunately, Mister Winston, I know exactly what you're talking about and you know exactly what I'm talking about."

She sat down and there was the thigh again. The thigh pressed too tightly to mine.

What do you do about a girl with lean flanks?

I was reminded of D. H. Lawrence and "The Horse-dealer's Daughter." And I was reminded that Nellie spelled trouble backwards. And I was reminded that that was the kind of thing she would have said. I didn't like to see my mind run in those channels. I had other responsibilities. Academic responsibility and psychological responsibility were horses—and horse dealers' daughters—of different colors.

I had her kicked out of school.

She didn't take it very well. She came into the office in a very lovely wool suit. It was navy blue and had brass buttons and a red lining. She said, "You see, Mister Winston, my family has loads and loads of money."

"It's very chic, Nellie."

"You stink, Mister Winston."

"I had no choice, Nellie."

"I've got no place to go now, Mister Winston, so whatever happens to me, good or bad, is your fault."

"Don't dramatize, Nellie."

"I want to dramatize. . . ."

"You can go to another university and reenter when you've shown your willingness. . . ."

"I think I've shown lots of willingness. . . ."

"Nellie. . . ."

"Call me Miss Patch."

"Not Mrs. Falkenheimer?"

"You *stink*."

I never knew what became of her, or where she went, or what had happened to her until one day, three years later, when she appeared in my office. She was much more beautiful than she had been as a child. She had acquired élan and resignation and excellent carriage.

"Hello, Mister Winston."

"Hello, Miss Patch."

"Still not Mrs. Falkenheimer?"

"All right, then, Mrs. Falkenheimer."

"Fooled you, as usual. It's not Mrs. Falkenheimer any more."

"What is it now?"

"Mrs. Brady—Mrs. John Brady, Jr."

I said, "Oh, you've married again," and she said that it was obvious and inevitable that she should and would marry again. She told me that once upon a time she would have liked to marry me because she thought she would have been a good teacher's wife.

She said, "I mean a *good* teacher's *wife*, not a *good teacher's* wife. Do you understand the difference? You're a lousy teacher. But I would have been a good wife, and a credit to you."

I thanked her.

She apologized, and then she laughed.

She told me not to be nervous because she wasn't going to make a pass at me. She told me that she wasn't in love with me any more, that she had outgrown me long since. And then she asked me if that was grammatical. I told her it was vaguely grammatical. She said that she was married to a very successful young actor who was in a Broadway play, and that he was John Brady, Junior, the Star. She said it as if it were all one name, John-Brady-Junior-the-Star . . . and that she had decided to go back to school in her spare time to read all those books. All the ones she planned to read before she died.

I must have shown some kind of anxiety because she put her hand on my cheek and she said, "Listen, I'm no longer what I used to be. I'm respectable now, respectable and married. It's terribly fashionable to be respectable and married and going back to school. I'm at General Studies. The Barnard bit was a bit much. I like it over at General Studies. The people that study there really come to study. And besides, you don't have to take gym."

She told me that she was going to study Ancient History because of Greece. She said that she thought they really had the message in the Periclean Age and asked didn't I agree. When I hesitated she said, "You were always stuck for an answer, Mister Winston."

I agreed. And I looked at her. She had what, for want of a better expression, was the Sweet Smell of Success, by the Movie of the Same Name. She had been places and seen things that you don't see in an office in Barnard College. I told her that she spoke as if she knew more of life than Marvell. (My thesis was on Marvell.) She asked me if I had finished my explication of "To His Coy Mistress." She quoted:

> "Had we but world enough, and time,
> This coyness, Lady, were no crime.

Or words to that effect? Kind of fits us, doesn't it?"

She wore an orange cashmere dress and an orange ribbon in her hair. It was wound twice around her head and tied in a knot that nestled in the left crook of her neck.

I must have been staring at the knot and the neck because she said, "Listen, Charlie—you were the one that was selling the Hemlock. Don't look back."

"Where did you disappear to?"

"I went out into the wide, wide world, just like Willie Loman's brother, and gathered up all the rhinestones. They're there for the asking."

"And now you've got a new husband and you say he's successful. . . ."

"And maybe soon we'll have a family. . . . Show and Tell Time?"

She unfolded her saga about becoming a singer and how she had even had a chance to become a movie star, and how she'd given it all up for love. Not for the love of her second husband. She said that no one worth their salt ever loved any husband. She told me she had given everything up for the love of a Writer. "The one that wrote the story," she said, "the story you read us in Freshman English class."

I didn't know which or what story she was talking about. She said that she had met the Writer in Boston and everything that happened with him was all because of me. She invited me to take her to lunch, and I took her to the Faculty Club. The Intermediate French Teacher looked at us askance.

Nellie just laughed.

That lunch was neither pleasant, nor unpleasant.

Nellie filled me in on her husband's career and progress. She spoke of him with a condescending affection. She spoke of him as if he were a puppet and she the puppetmaster. And the strange thing is, that she spoke of herself in the same way. Totally disassociated, totally disengaged. The beholder, the *deus ex machina* of her own existence.

"It's funny about me," she said, "I really ought to be

176

dead and buried or in the looney bin by now, and instead I always come up smelling like a rose. Maybe because I want to see the hand played out. You know, I never could walk out on anything. . . . I'll sit around till the end of the show and let life walk out on me. . . . *N'est-ce pas?*"

"Your life hasn't been any better or any worse than anybody else's, Nellie."

"That's not grammatical, Mister Winston."

I tried to explain that wanting to survive was neither unique nor shameful. Nellie answered that she didn't just want to survive. She wanted to survive in Spades.

She looked around the room and down at the gravy on her hot turkey sandwich. She started eating the mixed vegetables one by one with the prong of her fork.

"The Groves of Academe has never been famous for its cuisine."

I asked her if she'd prefer to go somewhere else, and she laughed. "Not on your life," she hissed. "Here I am with all you bums who had me booted out of school and I'm one up on all of you. I've been to London figuratively speaking, and seen the Queen. That French bitch can't take her eyes off my dress. Look at her, she knows I've got the world by the tail."

I choked on my mixed vegetables.

"Or I could say, My tail has always been my strong point, Mister Winston."

I asked her if she had come to be friends or if she had come for vengeance.

"Both. . . . No, not really both. Mostly to be friends . . . and to study Ancient History. . . . I think I'll do a paper on orgies. What do you think?"

"I think that you may have been to the Figurative London to see the Figurative Queen, but you're still Nellie Patch."

"Nellie Patch Falkenheimer Brady, Jr."

"You're still Nellie Patch who never forgave her father for marrying a woman from the Twin Cities. . . ."

"So you remembered."

"I remembered."

"Thank you for remembering."

"You're welcome."

"Can we have lunch again, Mister Winston?"

"Anytime."

"Next time, I'll take you. We'll go to the Russian Tea Room. My treat. We can have eggplant caviar and hot borscht and pirojoks."

I told her that for all her carrying on about sex, her true passion was food, but that I would accept the lunch with pleasure. She leaned over the table and the orange of the ribbon was picked up by all the highlights in her hair, and she put her hand to her face, and the orange was reflected in the gold of her wedding ring, and she said, "You still are very handsome in a booky way, Mister Winston."

"Thank you, Mrs. Brady."

I was on the Barnard side of Broadway and she was on the Columbia side, and we never ran into each other. I missed her, and I wondered about her. . . .

Then, two or three months later, I came into my office and found her sitting there. All her hair was piled into a black velvet hat and her neck looked three miles long. . . . Nefertiti in a toque. She said, "Guess what, Mister Winston? I'm back in the sack on the old mill stream, or rather, back in the sack on the shores of the old mill stream."

When I asked her what she meant she explained that her husband had gone to California and that she had decided not to go with him, not for any personal reasons, just because he wasn't a real husband and she wasn't a real wife. And then the neck arched with great pride, and she bit her lower lip and the glinted golden eyes filled with real tears, and she said, "Mister Winston, I hate studying Ancient History. The people were swingers, but the way they teach it, is so boring. I mean, we have to make maps and take quizzes on map-making. I wanted to study about the soul of the world, and instead, I'm learning cartography. . . . The cartography of boundaries that no longer exist. . . . Mister Winston—please invite me out for a cup of coffee?"

I said of course, and we walked out of the building and out onto Broadway.

There were all the slovenly Barnard girls in their dungarees and their sweaters and their raincoats looking at this elegant woman in the black velvet hat.

She looked back at them and said, "Which one is me, Mister Winston?"

We started to walk down the street and she said, "You know, I really don't want a cup of coffee. I want to get drunk. Let's go to the West End, okay?"

We walked down to the West End and sat at the bar while Nellie instructed the bartender as to how to make a proper martini. After the drinks had been made and poured, we carried them over to a booth and sat opposite each other. She stuck her tongue into her drink and winced. She said, "Either you have it or you don't. . . . I guess he doesn't."

She drank the drink in one gulp.

"He didn't remember me. That's sad, isn't it?"

"You look different."

"Only because I am."

She began to talk of her husband and his picture contract and about what a success he was going to be. There was a bitterness that had not been in her voice when she had first spoken of him. There was the old condescension and some vague overtones of pity. She said he had always bored her and her plan was that now he had gone to California, she would leave school.

The logic of this evaded me, and I tried to explain that for whatever reason or reasons she had broken her marriage, it didn't seem practical to leave school. It would be something to do.

She looked at me as if I were a fool, and she said, "Doperino, I only needed to have something to do when I was married so that I could have some place to go besides home. You know actors hang around the house all the time, especially when they're working. The only days I really had to myself were Wednesday and Saturdays—they're matinee days. Now I can stay home and sing—to myself—or to whoever wants to listen. . . . Would you like to listen?"

I asked what her parents were going to think of this second divorce.

She said, "Do you really want to know?"

"Yes."

She started with her stepmother. She said that as far as the lady from the Twin Cities was concerned she, Nellie, could go up in the Graf Zeppelin and the lady would be delighted, and that whatever delighted the lady delighted her father, and that her real mother was dead.

"My real mother. Did I tell you she did the Dutch Act? The slow and steady one. . . . My real mother's dead and to all intents and purposes—as far as I'm concerned —so's my father.

"My father lives for and with the lady from the Twin Cities, and he was never there for me when he had to be there. Except, of course, with the checkbook. That's really too bad too, you know, because I'm the kind of person that needs a strong father figure. And even when he was living at home with Mama he was never there. He loved her, but he didn't really like her, and I guess that's why I have no character and no stability and why I like older men like you, you know. Sometimes I think that my real problem is that neither of my husbands were older men."

"Don't you have a guardian?"

"Sure, I do. . . . His name is Jesus H. Christ."

"Nellie, how old are you?"

"Old."

"How old?"

"I've lied about it so much I always forget. . . ."

"You must have a birth certificate."

"Sure—and a driver's license and a passport. They all say I'm forty-leven. . . ."

She was on her third martini by now and she was getting drunk.

"Nellie, the drinking. . . ."

"Heaven, isn't it? Learned it all from Mama. Do you know she used to 'ply me with alcohol'? My own mother. My very own mother used to pour me a belt that could wash away a longshoreman. I guess she figured if she was going to go the way of all flesh, I should go too. . . . I love Samuel Butler, don't you?"

"Don't name-drop. . . ."

"When you got me bounced out of school, no one gave a damn . . . but me, and maybe you. . . ."

"I didn't get you bounced out of school. You got yourself bounced out of school. . . ."

"The rationalization of the guilty, eh what? Say twenty-three Hail Marys—and poof! You're a malted. Get two more martinis from that moron and tell him to leave out the vermouth."

I went to the bar and ordered the drinks. And I captured her reflection in the mirror. She was sitting in that plastic imitation-leather booth, her black velvet head tilted to one side. She didn't know that I was watching her, but her face had become suddenly and strangely childlike beneath the hat. Then she caught me staring at her, and I shall never forget how she smiled and waved and then took the hat off and let all her hair come tumbling out and down and how she ran her hands through that hair and then smiled again and made a gesture as if to pick up a cocktail and say where the hell were they?

We sat there and drank martinis all afternoon, and I learned a little more about the Odyssey of Nellie.

It seemed that when she had been asked to leave school she had telephoned her father in Minneapolis and had told him what had happened and asked him what she should do. He and his wife from the Twin Cities had told her—the wife was on the telephone extension, and could talk to her simultaneously—that to leave New York would be to admit failure. They had told her to stick it out. And when she asked, to stick what out where, they explained that she should arrange to enter Finch or N.Y.U. and bring up her grades and try to get back into Barnard, after showing her mettle.

She thanked them for the check they were sending and called her mother in St. Louis. Her mother's brother answered. He said that her mother was back in the booby hatch for one of her drying outs and that it was absolutely revolting of her to have done something as dumb as be kicked out of school. He said if she came home to St. Louis everyone would know she had been kicked out of school, and that just wouldn't do. He said that she should immediately go to the Classified Directory and find a good secretarial school and enroll there, and learn to support herself like a decent human being. She thanked him for the check that he was sending, and that's when she met Mike Isaacs and tootled down the road to hell.

"Instead of being a secretary, like my avuncular uncle

suggested, I became a naked model. It set the pattern for my future. You know, I sometimes wonder if there may have been some action between my mother and her brother . . . why else was she so flippy?"

"And the singing, Nellie?"

"The singing was for the birds. . . ."

"Not really."

"Of course, not really. The singing was really real. . . . Listen, would you like to come home with me? And make love to me? In show business when people make love in the afternoon they refer to it as a matinee, so if you'd like a matinee, I'm scale and avail. That, my Academician, is a show-business term that means I get low pay and I'm at liberty. And absolutely cramped up with lust for you. So let's have it over with, *n'est-ce pas?* A three-year lust . . . for a teacher, yet."

I told her that I knew all about matinees, and that it was bad form to solicit.

"Why, Mister Winston. . . . I do believe that you've gone and passed Intermediate French. An earnest young actress? No? Yes. An earnest young actress, and you helped her with the interpretation of all the Classics. An earnest young actress who's left you and gone to California?"

I didn't answer.

"Mister Winston, darling, we're in the same boat. And we both know firsthand about matinees. But I know something you don't know. I know about nooners. Etymologically speaking, Mister Winston, think on nooners."

I told her that I didn't have to think, and that I knew all about nooners.

"But you should think, Mister Winston. Because it's an interesting question of usage. In New York we have matinees, but in California they all get up at dawn and they become oriented to an earlier lunch, so they have nooners . . . fascinating insight into etymology, no?"

She told me the reason she knew all about nooners was because she could have been one, but that she hadn't become one because she was a nice girl.

"I am a nice girl aren't I? Am I not? Which is grammatical, Mister Winston?"

"Am I not."

"*Am I Not a Nooner?* by Nellie Patch. 'Twould be a best-seller, Mister Winston. The confessions of a whore written by a Nice Girl."

I told her that if she wanted to be a nice girl she'd better act like one and stop talking as if she were a tramp.

"Always the subjunctive, Mister Winston?"

She sang,

> "*I don't care . . . what Ma-ma says . . . now.*
> *I'm going to . . . shake it any-how.*
> *I'm going to shimmy like my sister Kate. . . .*"

She was very drunk and trying not to cry. She said, "Mister Winston, if you have any love or pity in your heart, come home with me. I'm so different from the Nellie that got kicked out of school. I lost her, and maybe you're the only one in the world that can help me find her again. I'm not anything like I was when you met me and I know things and I've seen things that would make you flip your lid. So come home with me, Mister Winston, and leave your cheap edicts on behavior wagging behind you, and don't tell me about nice girls and not nice girls, because girls are girls, Mister Winston. They're what other people make them . . . and when other people make them—the girls, not the edicts—they're *not* nice girls according to the people that make them."

I paid the bill and took her home. Home was on Central Park West. It was an eight-room apartment with four bathrooms, and a stereophonic record-player system that reverberated through all the rooms.

We walked into the front hall and Nefertiti—she had put the toque back on—Nefertiti hollered, "Maude?" A very nice-looking colored woman came out of the kitchen and Nellie said, "Maude—this is Mister Winston. He's going to board here for a while."

"Yes, Mrs. Brady."

"Be nice to him, Maude. Because if you're nice to him, he'll be nice to me."

I told Maude to make a pot of coffee and Maude nodded philosophically and said, "Yes sir, Mister Winston."

We went into the living room and sat down. Nellie told me that she was delighted that I had taken the initiative in asking Maude to make the coffee. She said that was what was awful about living with an actor. You had to do everything yourself. It was boring.

She smoked two cigarettes and didn't say anything. I looked around at the living room, and I looked at her . . . Nellie Brady. Nellie Patch. Nellie Falkenheimer. Nellie, an inevitable phenomenon of American society. . . . A built-in victim. Hoisted on her own petard. . . .

After she had finished the second cigarette, she invited me into the Master Bedroom. The bed was the focal point of the decor. There were many clocks and chests and chairs, but the bed dominated. She took off all her clothes and laid them neatly on a chaise longue. Then she stood on tiptoes and said, "Now what, Mister Winston, Mister Winston, Mister Winston . . . ? Mister Winston Sir. . . ."

We used to play Categories with a capital C. Nellie said she loved it, because it had been President Kennedy's favorite game. We used to play in bed, always for money. She always cheated and she always won. Maude would bring us coffee in bed, and look at us with disdain. Nellie loved patterns. It was Categories and Maude and champagne and black coffee. In the morning I would go up to Barnard and Nellie would go to visit the painter named Mike Isaacs.

"I like to visit Mike, he thinks about me like I used to be before. Before all the bad things happened. You know, Mister Winston, nobody cared what happened to me but Mike Isaacs, and his only problem was that he was a lousy lay. If he were not—dig the subjunctive—I would be with him, not you, Mister Winston. You know what I want you to do?"

"What do you want me to do?"

"I want you to write on me."

"With what?"

"Lipstick."

"Nellie, I once told you not to dramatize. . . ."

"Mister Winston—do you know why I go to visit Mike Isaacs? I go to visit him because . . . he knew me when I was a 'tabula rasa'—a slate which has never been written upon, but does get written upon, and once having been written upon, is no longer a 'tabula rasa,' so it can be written upon again and again, and again. So write on me, Charlie. Write on my breasts and on my belly and on my behind. Okay? And I want you to write in lipstick because that'll make it seem like kisses."

I wrote on her. I wrote, "Stay slim and beautiful," on her belly—and I wrote, "The cheekiest of cheek" on her behind—and I wrote "Bonne Femme, Bonne Femme," on each of her breasts, and she roared with laughter because it tickled and she ran naked to the mirror to read all the writing.

"Each one is a *bon mot*, Mister Winston . . . *merci mille fois*. . . ." Then she took Kleenex and baby oil and erased all the writing, saying, "The moving hand writes and having writ moves on." She said that she had quoted it incorrectly and that she never got lyrics right. She said, "It's like '*Mene, mene, tekel, mene, mene, tekel, oo fah sun.*' That's from the Old Testament and it means, 'All your days are numbered days.' See, I did learn some ancient history, Mister Winston, but not at school."

I chose not to answer.

"My mother always told me that cleanliness was next to Godliness, that's why I'm erasing myself."

She hollered for Maude. Maude came into the bedroom.

"Maude, we want coffee and cinnamon toast. Double-quick, Maudie!"

Maude went to fix the coffee and cinnamon toast, and Nellie went into the bar and got a bottle of champagne and brought two glasses. She always kept champagne on ice. She said it was our one vital household staple. She asked me to please uncork it. I drank the coffee and ate the cinnamon toast. She drank the champagne.

She said, "You'll never guess what we're celebrating, Mister Winston."

"What are we celebrating, Nell?"

"We're celebrating the anniversary of the death of my baby. . . ."

I told her that I didn't know that she had lost a baby and I asked her if that was why her marriage had broken up.

"Which marriage, Mister Winston?"

"The second marriage, Nellie."

"God, you're dumb, Mister Winston. Of course nobody like me could ever get pregnant from an actor. I got pregnant in Boston, Mister Winston, from the Writer, from the one I really love. And you know what? I never told, but I had the abortion on Valentine's Day. Frank Cos-

tello or the other one—Al Capone—and me—me or I?—
and me, we have something in common. A sentiment for
Valentine's Day. I chose to have the abortion on Valentine's Day because it would be memorable and a mas-
sacre, and so I wouldn't forget. I mean after all, it's not
good form to forget that kind of thing."

She took a big swig of the champagne from the bottle
and then she leaned over and poured it from her mouth
to mine. . . . "Very classy artificial respiration, Mister
Winston?" I told her it was very classy.

She went on to say that she was very glad that she had
had the Valentine's Day abortion because she would
have a real baby now and wouldn't that be a drag? A drag
on both of us.

I told her that the tough facade was wearing pretty
thin and she asked me why didn't I leave her. I was stuck
for an answer. I didn't leave because I had grown to love
all the clocks and all the hunt tables, and Maude's pious
looks. I had grown to love Jack Buchanan's old records
and I had grown to wait for the sweet, sweet moments
when my thin-facaded friend sat on the piano and sang
for me. And I didn't leave because I was afraid of what
would happen to her if I did.

And so in lieu of an answer I poured myself a glass of
champagne and held it in my mouth and leaned over and
poured it into hers.

She swallowed the champagne and she held onto me,
and she said, "Make me a baby. You know why my real
baby died? You know why? Because nobody ever really
wanted me to have a baby except me. . . . And maybe
you? Nobody else ever wanted me to have a baby except
me, because nobody except me and maybe you ever
really trusted me."

I told her that I couldn't make her a baby because I
wasn't her husband.

She said, "If that's a proposal and you're trying in some sneaky way to ask me to marry you, I'll say, 'Thank you very much, but no thank you. You see, I've had two, sir, and it's not polite to take a third.' Do you know what they do to you after you've been a four-time loser? They sentence you to life or death, whichever is worse. They punish you for all the bad things you've ever done. That's what they did to my mother. They made her do the Dutch Act for all the bad things she'd done."

When I asked her who "they" were, she said, "They're after us. Hide with me under the covers and let's do bad things where they can't see us. Know what I mean?"

I asked her why she always punctuated every sentence with "know what I mean?"

"Because I always think no one listens, or understands what I'm talking about."

"Why?"

"Because I don't understand what I mean or what I'm talking about, and if I don't how can anybody else?"

"Okay. You win. Let's do bad things."

"Under the covers?"

"Anywhere you say."

"I say the Uffizi Gallery in Florence. That's where Botticelli's Venus lives. . . . Take me there. . . ."

"All right—I'm taking you there. . . . I'm taking you there. . . ."

"Am I now in the Uffizi Gallery and doing bad things right beneath the presence of the Botticelli Venus?"

"Yes."

"Who's prettier, she or me?"

"She's dead and you're alive, so you're prettier."

"Bastard."

Bastard or not, I thrived. There had been other girls and other women, of course. Nellie had been quite right in her prognostication. I had passed Intermediate French and gone on to off-Broadway. And I had tasted on-Broadway more than once, and on-Park Avenue only once—or twice.

I used to know a Dane who would say, "For a man all the world is a smorgasbord. You take some herring, some smoked eel, a little bit of aspic. You try the Italian salami, the head cheese, the smoked cheese, the Danish ham, the coarse pâté, and the fine pâté, and the mussels. You take the Bibb lettuce and avocado, and then you go on to the meatballs, sweet and sour, and you take more salad and more aspic, and cold beans and cold beets. . . . The secret is only to taste. And finally, you know what you want? You want to eat, not to taste. But you're full, and you have to wait till next time."

Nellie was my next time. I wanted to partake of nubescent flesh and vintage wine. I, the scholar in spite of himself, the teacher stuffed with himself, the lover in lieu of the Lover. And bastard or not, I thrived on good living . . . and felt that I was doing my share to contribute to Nellie's necessities.

Academy Award nomination time tolled around and John Brady, Jr., won a nomination for Best Actor. Nellie smirked and said, "*Ça va sans dire.* He's going to win." She said that she couldn't wait for the presentations. She said that she hoped that Richard would be there because then he would see that she really was Rapunzel and she could spin gold from straw. I told her that she had her wires crossed, and it was Rumpelstiltskin, a hunchedbacked dwarf, who could spin gold from straw, and that he did it all for the love of the Miller's Daughter.

"And Rapunzel?"

"Rapunzel let her hair down so the Prince could climb to the Tower in which she was kept prisoner."

"Was she kept prisoner for doing bad things?"

"No! She was kept prisoner in order that she wouldn't do bad things."

"But the Prince?"

I explained to her that the Prince was chivalrous and used to climb up to the Tower just to read poetry and sing love ballads, and she told me that the Prince didn't have to climb all the way up to a Tower to do that, and added that I had never known how to interpret literature.

She had a point.

I would sit before my Seventeenth Century class and attempt to analyze John Donne and the sexual symbolism of his passion for God, and think of my passion for champagne and Maude and Nellie, and I would sit before my Freshman English class and wonder whether or not John Brady, Jr., was going to win the Academy Award.

Nellie was totally confident of his chances. I kept analyzing his chances the way a compulsive gambler works on a scratch sheet.

The head of the English Department called me into his office and told me he had heard rumors that I'd been distracted of late. I told him it was pressure, the pressure of finishing my thesis. He accepted that with a gratuitous and undoubtedly ironic, "Delighted to know you've come to the end of the road."

The night of the Academy Awards we climbed into bed, turned on the television, and uncorked the champagne.

Nellie wore a black lace nightgown and wound a black ribbon twice around her hair. She said it was only fitting that she dress formally for the occasion.

She explained to me that the awards would either go all for one picture or else be spread across the board, and it turned out to be one of those years when they were spread across the board.

I was on tenterhooks. I don't know why. I didn't give a damn for John Brady, Jr., or the Academy of Motion Picture Arts and Sciences.

Nellie was serene. She sat up in bed and drank her champagne and waited stoically until they announced that John Brady, Jr., had won the award for Best Actor of the Year. She turned to me and said, "I guess there must be a Rumpelstiltskin in my life. I guess he spun gold from straw . . . but not for the Miller's Daughter, darling— for the butcher's daughter."

She got up and whipped off the television just as Brady began his acceptance speech. She said, "Who needs to hear it? He's going to thank the director and the writer and the technicians and Nat Gench when he should really be thanking Rumpelstiltskin. . . . Hey, listen . . . if I let my hair down will you climb into my Tower?"

"To read poetry and sing love ballads?"

"You read the poetry. I'll sing the love ballads."

She got out of bed and dragged me into the living room and pushed me down on the sofa—and she screamed for Maude—once, twice, three times she hollered for Maude, and poor Maude came running out of her room in her flannel nightgown with what is known as a "wrapper" clutched to her bosom and Nellie said, "Maude, sit next to Mister Winston. You're going to be the audience."

She climbed up on top of the piano, sat down, composed herself and said, "Ladies and gentlemen, my name is Nellie, and while I'm waiting for the sun to shine I'm going to sing for you." She said, "You see, that's the way the act started—simply. I would begin with 'Why Was I Born'?—

Why was I born?
Why am I living?

192

What do I get?
What am I giving. . . ."

She finished the song, shrugged her shoulders and then started

"Maybe I'm right
And maybe I'm wrong,
And maybe I'm weak
And maybe I'm strong,
But nevertheless——"

She stopped herself.

"Nevertheless, I'm the one that should have been the star. Not that moron. Right?"

I told her that if she really wanted to have been a star, she could have been one. And she said, "No. No. Never! Can't you hear it? Can't you hear it, or do you have a tin ear? Can't you hear that I can't make the sound and I can't even fake it? It's too late for me. I can't make the sound any more."

She turned on Maude and said, "What the hell are you doing here? What do you think this is, a peep show?"

Maude said, "Good night, Mister Winston." She just looked at Nellie. She went back to her room.

Nellie uncorked another bottle of champagne and said, "I bet she leaves me tomorrow." She drank the champagne right from the bottle, and then she unwound the black ribbon and told me to climb up to the Tower, and when I started to take off her black lace nightgown she threw her head back with something like disdain and said, "God, I hope that Richard was there."

One night, late in May, I came to the apartment only to be let in by Maude who served me a sullen and cold supper. She told me that Mrs. Brady was at Mr. Isaacs' apartment and that Mrs. Brady had left instructions that I be fed cold chicken and sliced tomatoes. I ate what was put before me, and just as I reached the thigh of the bird Nellie burst in and said, "You'll never guess what . . . Mike says that Richard called him and said he's coming to New York, and Mike said that Richard said he wanted to know how to get in touch with me and wanted to know if I was listed in the phone book or could he give him my phone number, and Mike said that he wants to see me . . . and you see, you see, I told you it would all work out."

I asked her what would work out.

She said, "Mister Winston, don't you understand Richard liberated me. He liberated me from being a middle-class slob, and he's the most important person in my life, and the reason I've never been able to have him until now is because I didn't deserve him. I was always penny ante."

She talked on and on about Boston and Hollywood, and then I understood why I could never have her. She said that only Tangible Accomplishment could make one worthy of love, and that goodness, virtue, honesty were nothing without Tangible Accomplishment. She cited her Tangible Accomplishment—one John Brady, Jr.

And with that accomplishment her great passion could and would commence.

She was very polite about telling me to get myself and all my things out of her apartment. I told her that I would do so as quickly as possible, and I went in to the bedroom to get the few books and clothes that I had there. She followed right behind me and said, "Of course, you'll be reachable in case I need you."

I tried to explain to her that Tangible Accomplishment or not you don't treat people as if they had no feeling for

194

you or pride in themselves. Of course, her answer was pure and simple Nellie logic.

"People treat me as if they have no feeling for me and I've never found anything to feel proud of myself for. The only thing I've learned is that in this world it's each man for himself. I never used to believe that—till I got smart. And it's important that Richard doesn't know you've been living here because if he did know he'd be jealous."

I asked her how she could believe that a man could be jealous when he hadn't bothered to get in touch with her for over a year, even though he undoubtedly knew she'd been separated and she said that it was just the kind of love affair that a person like me could never understand.

"You see, one night when we were in the hospital, Richard promised to make me happy. He promised me that if I was a good girl and I grew up to be a beautiful woman and to accomplish things he would leave his wife and marry me. And when I asked him how I would know when I was good and beautiful and a woman who had accomplished things, he said I would know it when I had a sense of myself.

That night, when we were in the hospital, he said— not sang, he said,

" 'Wait till the sun shines, Nellie.' You know how it goes?

> *Wait till the sun shines, Nellie*
> *Till the clouds go rolling by*
> *We could be so happy, Nellie*
> *Sweetheart, you and I.*
> *Down lover's lane we'll wander*
> *Hush now, don't you cry*
> *Just wait till the sun shines, Nellie*
> *Bye and bye.*

195

"You see—he got it—he understood. I have the true sense of myself now and I think I'm as good and beautiful as a woman can be expected to be, and I have tangible proof of accomplishment. After all, my friend, you saw Mr. Star yourself on the old television winning the Academy Award, and you don't think it was his Aunt Sadie that led him down the garden path to that. I've paid my dues, Mister Winston. I've paid all the dues I've ever had to pay to deserve Richard. And Rumpelstiltskin didn't spin the straw for me. I spun it for myself."

When I asked her why she felt it was necessary to pay dues to deserve Richard she sat up very straight and very still and said, "In each man or woman's life you pay your money and you take your choice. It's always illogical, but Richard is my choice. He was the first man that ever counted for anything, so he is Mr. Big. He's the man. I see him in color. Before him it was always ersatz color, and even though it's nice with you, I love Richard. You see, he writes and you teach—you know, baby, those who can, do, and those who can't, teach."

I felt that the world had gone mad, and so had she.

I had never met Richard Timon but there was not one shred of evidence, not one fact, not one image, not one impression to make me think he was anything but a facile and banal young man who had managed to graduate from popular literary magazines to even more popular motion pictures. He had the ability to cram the maw of the public's desire for popcorn and Milky Ways, but to Nellie he was God.

So I packed my things to leave and I knew that I would be called or fallen upon—if I were lucky. Just before I got through the front door, she called to me. She said, "Mister Winston, are you really going to leave without kissing me goodbye?"

Of course I kissed her goodbye. She looked up at me

196

and she said, "You know a terrible thing, Mister Winston. I'm afraid of birds because I think I'm like one. I think someday I'll go crazy like a bird goes crazy in a cage or in a house and I'll start to smash myself against the walls."

You don't walk out when someone says something like that to you. And I took her two hands in mine and led her to the sofa, and I said, "Nellie, tell me something—when you say you have a 'sense of self'—the sense of self that's so important to Richard—what is it that you mean?"

"A sense of self is being whole and real and not having to feed off other peoples' insides.

> *Free an' easy*
> *That's my style*
> *Howdy do-dee*
> *Watch me smile.*

Do you understand? When you have a sense of self 'anyplace you hang your hat is home' you know, like the song, and what Richard wanted was for me not to be so dependent . . . on him or on images."

"And now you're not dependent?"

"No, I'm not. So I can have him. It is weird though, I admit, when I was dependent and I really needed him to come through for me he wouldn't have me . . . and now that I'm independent and good and beautiful, and an accomplished woman, I'm going to have him. Timing is so funny, isn't it? It's the whole secret. God knows, we'd all be better off if we'd synchronize our watches. . . . Like you and me. When I was in school and needed you, you didn't want me, and maybe if you had, nothing bad would have happened to me, but now it's you that wants me, and it's me that's telling you no."

I wished her good luck and left. And I waited.

197

Sure enough, ten days later she called and said, "Hey? This is Nellie, please come home. Even though you're not Bill Bailey."

I vaguely know what Moral Rearmament is all about. I understand it's vaguely Right Wing, but I did know I needed some kind of Rearmament, and even though I had never met the man, I decided to call Mike Isaacs. I knew that he was Nellie's confidant and that whatever I had confided to her was privy to him and that he would know exactly who I was and what I was, and probably much more about me than I cared to have known by anyone, especially a stranger. But there was, to put it euphemistically, a bond between us.

I telephoned him, gave my name, and asked if I might talk to him about Nellie Patch.

He invited me to his studio, offered me a drink, showed me a chair, and I sat down and faced a painting of a beautiful girl with no face—the famous faceless portrait of Nellie.

I just said, "What happened?"

He said, "Did she ask you to come back to her?"

"Yes."

"Are you going?"

"Should I?"

He said, "That's your problem, not mine."

"Who is Timon, anyway?"

"A mutual friend of Nellie's and mine."

I didn't think that was very funny and he knew I didn't. Then he told me what had happened.

Nellie had come running to his studio. She was high enough when she arrived but really staggering when they left for the airport to pick up Timon. He poured containers of black coffee into her in the cab, and when they got to Kennedy she had achieved a minimal level of sobriety.

But she was trembling with excitement and fear, and then he stopped his recitation for a moment and said, "Wonderful, isn't it, the way she tells you all about how she feels about him?"

I didn't have to answer, so he went on with his story. He said the three of them went to the Russian Tea Room and ate and drank, and Nellie couldn't keep her hands off Timon. She kept trying to hold his hand or put her arm around his neck or sit too close to him. He said Timon wallowed in all of it, especially in all the other people in the restaurant watching this beautiful girl throw herself at him.

They left the Tea Room and he dropped them both at Nellie's apartment and went home. The next morning Nellie called his studio to say she had woken up and he was gone.

Isaacs said he doesn't know whether he did it to get even, and if it was, he didn't know for what, but he asked her who was gone, and she screamed, "Who the hell do you think is gone—Santa Claus?"

He made us both another drink and I remember thinking to myself, "Who the hell do you think is gone—Santa Claus?" said it all. All the toughness, the facade, the girl who couldn't make the sound, the bird that was going to fly into a wall were all there in "Who the hell do you think is gone—Santa Claus?"

He said he had gone right over to her apartment and that the place was a wreck, and that she was pacing the floor and crying like a spoiled child, shrieking at Maude, guzzling champagne. He took Maude into the kitchen and told her to make a pot of coffee, and Maude broke down and said she didn't know how she was going to stand it any more. She said Nellie'd been on the telephone all morning calling every hotel in New York, asking if Timon was there and screaming at the hotels when

199

they told her that he wasn't, screaming that they were lying to her, that they'd better put her through or they'd be sorry. Maude said she even called Timon's wife and cursed her out on the phone.

He told me he went back into the living room and Nellie wasn't there so he went into the bedroom and he found her sitting on the bed hugging her pillow and keening like an Irish widow, saying, "Why, why, why, why, why, why?"

He stayed with her all morning, finally got her to swallow a sedative, and when she fell asleep he left and went to see Timon.

The explanation to "why?" was very simple. Timon had really wanted to see Nellie, but he didn't want to be caught walking out of her apartment building in the morning. He knew too many people who lived in the neighborhood. He had had every intention of seeing her again. But now, he didn't know. He was furious that she'd called his wife. He had enough problems to straighten out with his wife without having Nellie calling to make them this specific.

I asked him where he'd found Timon.

He smiled at me and said, "He's staying with me."

At this point I must have looked a little surprised because he said, "I told you he was a friend of mine. Long before he was a friend of Nellie's. . . ."

"And he's left his wife?"

"For the time being."

"Then what happened?"

What happened was what always happened with Nellie and Timon. She sobered up, she forgot, she forgave, and when he came back to see her again three days later she welcomed him with open arms and a cold bottle of Cordon Rouge 880. That was the last time she saw him before he left, and Isaacs told her to consider herself very lucky.

He said, "You have to understand Timon, to understand that he didn't know he was being cruel. He didn't come to New York just to see Nellie. And he would have seen her more often if she had been on good behavior."

Isaacs went on to explain that Timon was on his way to Rome to do a picture and wanted to use the ten days between planes to see Nellie, but that he—being Timon—had other things to do, other people to see. He wanted to use the ten days between planes to straighten things out with his wife and leave a berth open to be able to come back in case he changed his mind about the divorce. Isaacs said Nellie was lucky that her little phone call to his wife hadn't blacklisted her for good. Then he added that Timon had also wanted to shore up connections with a sideline attraction he had made in Hollywood after his Italian had said, "*Ciao.*" Timon never burned his bridges.

And "Dear Nell" was still one of his bridges, and she had gotten first honors, but ought to have known that she had to wait her turn to come up to bat again. Very simple. He had been polite enough to call Nellie to say goodbye, to tell her that he would write to her, to tell her that she should write to him, to suggest that she come to Rome for a holiday and to be sure to look him up if she did. If not, he'd be sure to call her when he came back to New York.

I asked Isaacs, "Why Timon?" and Isaacs just looked at me and said, "Why you and not me?"

I went back to my office and tried correcting papers and had a conference with one of my Freshman English students who looked at me with soulful adoration, and I wondered why she didn't press her thigh against mine

201

and make it unnecessary for me to return to Mrs. John Brady, Jr., but the extent of the Freshman's adoration was spiritual and intellectual, both in process and content. Every year you get older and every year the girls are the same age, and this girl was just a Freshman and Nellie was Nellie. So I locked my office and went back to the apartment on Central Park West.

She opened the door with great dignity and graciousness. The First Lady inviting you to enter the Blue Room. The place was spotless. Maude had obviously stayed through thick and thin. Nellie was immaculate, dressed in a white sharkskin sheath. She offered me coffee. I thanked her, and she called to Maude in dulcet tones and asked her to bring the coffee. Maude brought coffee on a silver tray and Nellie poured a cup for me. I reached out for it and very politely she poured it all over my hand and said, "You dirty son of a bitch! How dare you go and visit Mike Isaacs?"

If I had been smart I would have walked right out then and there. Instead I went into the bathroom, to get the coffee off and came back, not to the First Lady but to an absolutely livid Nellie.

She said, "How dare you meddle in parts of my life that don't belong to you?"

"I've always thought your life was in the public domain."

"I haven't been dead long enough."

"But you're working on it."

"Don't say that!"

"What should I say?"

"Say how glad you are to be back."

"How can I say that when I'm not sure if I mean it?"

"Same way I say things when I'm not sure whether or not I mean them."

"I'm not you."

"Thank God."

"How did you find out I went to see Isaacs?"

"People tell people things, Jerkerino. . . . They call people on the telephone and they tell them things. He told me you asked whether or not you should come back to me."

"That's right."

"What'd he say?"

"He said, 'That's your problem, not mine.' "

She scratched the bridge of her nose and bit her upper lip, and then she tossed her head back and said, "He got that from Richard, you know."

"No, I didn't know."

"Richard was pretty lousy to me."

"Not enough Tangible Accomplishments?"

"Very funny."

"Not very funny at all."

"Listen, Mister Winston, you know and I know that the bastard walked out on me, but what you don't know is that I'm never going to give him another chance to do it again. I'm through with him for good. . . . He's nothing but a two-bit Hollywood hack and the only reason I've hung on this long is because I had a crush on him at a very vulnerable time in my life and created a mystique that was based on nothing but dross."

"Well said."

"Thank you. And welcome home. . . . Would you like some brandy with your coffee? You'll get it in a glass, not on your hand."

She put on the beseeching little-girl look, threw her arms around me and said, "Mister Winston, Mister Winston, Mister Winston—I'm so glad you decided to come back."

She kissed me dozens of times and then she sprang up and threw her arms out wide, and then pretended to stand at attention.

"I'm going to be on good behavior now. No more psychodrama. Just love and good times . . . you'll see."

That's exactly what I was thinking: "I'll see. . . ."

She pulled out a bottle of Courvoisier and poured some into an enormous snifter and handed it to me and poured some into a whiskey-sour glass for herself.

"I know it's very chic to do all that warming and sniffing, but frankly I think it's a bore. Cheers."

"Cheers."

"To good behavior."

"And to happy days."

"Then you'll stay. . . ."

"I'll stay. . . ."

"Hooray!"

She drank her brandy in one gulp and poured herself another, then came over and lay down on the sofa and put her head in my lap. "I've got to tell you something awful."

"What?"

"I called my husband."

"What for?"

"For more money."

"Is he giving it to you?"

"Of course he is."

"Good for you."

"Bad for you . . . very bad . . . a failing grade for you, Mister Winston. How can you know so much and not understand me? You know I'd never call to ask for more money. I called to ask him to take me back. . . . No comment, Mister Winston? I called to ask him to take me back and guess what? He wants a divorce. . . . I don't fit the image of the Academy Award Winner's wife. . . ."

I set the brandy down on the table and I stared into those glinty golden eyes, and then I just got up, and when I did she fell on the floor. But I just kept moving for the door and then I heard her laughing and laughing, and through the laughter she said, "No, no! I was only teasing. I was only teasing to see if you really cared and you do. . . . Come back, please. . . . I promise not to do it again. You fell for it, but I only did it to see if you cared." And more laughter. "I only did it to see if you cared. . . ." And then tears. . . . "I only did it to see if you cared. . . ."

So I came back and I picked her off the floor and I carried her into the bedroom and put her on the bed, and I held her with one arm and I took off her stockings with one hand, and she crooned to me, "You know, you know I would never call Brady for anything. . . . You know, you know I just said what I said to see if you cared—and you do care, don't you? Don't you? Show me how much you care. Take me to the Uffizi. . . . Climb into my Tower. . . . Help me. . . . Help me. . . ."

There is a poem by William Butler Yeats called "The Second Coming." I always read it to my Freshman English classes. It begins:

> *"Turning and turning in the widening gyre*
> *The falcon cannot hear the falconer;*
> *Things fall apart, the centre cannot hold. . . ."*

That's where I was. Turning round and round in the centre of the widening gyre.

If you were just a stranger looking in on us, you would

have said that things were very much the same as they had been before the ten-day hiatus created by Timon. The only external difference was that the bottles next to the bed were brandy bottles, not champagne bottles.

It was exam time, and I still went up to school every day. I had examinations to administer, papers to read and grade, young ladies to see, advise and categorize. I still worked on Marvell. No, I hadn't finished.

But Nellie was different. She became virtually paralyzed except for bed and brandy. She slept until two or three in the afternoon and then made Maude fix something nauseatingly wrong for her to eat—blini with caviar and sour cream, mousaka, coquille St. Jacques, prune and apricot mousse. Maude would stand with the patience of Job, the *Gourmet Cookbook* propped up in front of her, and follow the directions to the letter. When the book said, as it often does, "Do such-and-such according to your own discretion," Nellie would leap into the breach with advice.

Of course, when it was all done and garnished and served at the dining table she would take two bites and say, "It's really delicious, perfection, dear Maudie, but I'm full, full to the gills. You eat some and save the rest for Mister Winston."

Sometimes she would wash her hair and watch television while she dried it, and when the hair was dry she would dress herself and walk all the way up to the University and listen to *Otello* on the earphone apparatus they had in the Music Library. She said that everyone thought *Aïda* was Verdi's masterpiece, but it was just "Funiculi, Funicula" next to *Otello*.

Once she walked all the way down to the Doubleday Book Store on Fifty-second and Fifth and found a Helen Morgan record and took it into the listening booth and played it over and over and sang with it. That night she told me what she had done and hung her head in shame.

"I never *imitated* before. . . . I mean, I never copied . . . I just sang *like* her, not *copied*. . . . But I thought it would help me to find the sound."

"Did you find it?"

"I found her sound . . . but that's hers . . . it's mine I'm looking for."

"Sing for me?"

"No. . . ."

She rarely went to visit Isaacs. She still talked of him with affection, but she told me that my knowing him had ruined the whole thing for her. That he wasn't her own compartment now, because I knew him. . . .

She never talked about Timon, but she watched for the mail. . . . I wonder if she really expected a letter.

Everything was done lethargically. Everything but bed and brandy.

When the weather turned warm she would go up to the roof of the apartment building and sit in the sun, but she soon decided that what with the soot and the smog she was turning green instead of tan and she crawled back inside.

She said to me, "What are we going to do this summer?"

I told her I was going to Yaddo.

"What's that?"

"It's an artist's retreat in Saratoga Springs."

"You're not an artist."

"The people at Yaddo think I come within their definition of artist."

"Can I come?"

"No."

"Why?"

"Because they don't even allow you to have wives, much less——"

"Much less to have nooners?"

"I didn't mean it that way, Nell. What I meant was it's set up to create an atmosphere of total solitude in which one can——"

"Screw the lady artists?"

"In which one can do one's work undisturbed."

"Well, if one is so disturbed that one cannot do one's work I'll tell one what I think one should do. . . ."

"Nellie!"

"And I'll tell one what I've been thinking. . . ." She turned on me with such hatred and venom as I have never seen and said, "You really are a first-class nothing. I mean, if I were you I'd hate me. If I were you I'd say, 'What do you think I am, a yo-yo?' If I were you I'd pack up and get the hell out of here. . . . Sam, Harry, George, Max, Charlie Brown, whatever your name is. . . . If I were you I'd know that every time you make love to me I pretend it's Richard. If I were you I'd be ashamed of what I'm doing. . . . Get out of here, you bum. You're committing adultery with a bona fide married woman!"

So I left, and eight days later Mike Isaacs called me to say that the police had called him to tell him to go down to Roosevelt Hospital because there had been an "accident" and that the victim of the accident had told them to get in touch with him because he would know what to do if she died and if she didn't. When he got to the hospital it was only to identify a body that belonged to one Nellie Brady.

He told me that they said she had broken a beer bottle on a bar and slashed her wrists and cut her jugular vein and somehow, in some crazy way, had fallen on the jagged bottle and had gotten it right in the belly. He told me that he had called John Brady, Jr., and that Brady was flying East with his agent, but that in the meantime he told Mike to take care of things. Isaacs said he was still at the hospital, and would I please come down because there were a lot of questions that the police were asking, and he couldn't answer them and maybe I could.

So I went to the Roosevelt Hospital and I asked if I could see her, and the nurse explained that she was dead, and I had to say that I wanted to see her anyway. Because I did.

I don't know—I always thought those things were automatic—but with Nellie they didn't cover her face with the sheet. There was the face—perfect, untouched, no makeup, and I swear to God, half smiling, as if she had fooled us all.

There was a young Negro boy there. He had been in the bar when it happened. The police had questioned him and had finished with him, but he still hadn't gone home.

Even in death, she had the ability to make you linger.

I spoke with the police, told them what I knew. I told them I would be able to get correct information from the college files, information as to her family. . . . Of course, they asked why? Why she did it.

Of course there was nothing to say but, "Because. . . ."

"Was she depressed?"

"Yes."

"Had she had a sudden shock?"

"Her life had been a series of sudden shocks, mostly self-induced."

They asked nonsensical questions.

We gave equally nonsensical answers.

When they had finished with us we walked outside with the young colored boy and asked him to tell us how it happened.

He told us that she had come into a bar on Ninth Avenue in the Fifties, and that everybody knew she didn't belong there because of the way she was dressed and the way she looked and the way she carried herself. He said she was stoned, but not sloppy drunk. He said she carried herself like a lady. He said she pushed her way over to the bar and got right up and sat on the bar, and she started singing all the old-timey songs. He said she had leaned down and asked him if she was making the sound and he told her that it sounded pretty good to him. He said she drank vodka and beer and vodka and beer, and that she was drinking the beer right out of the bottle. And when we asked why nobody stopped her he said that she was pretty and that the singing was great and that everybody was getting a charge out of her.

"But then," he said, "then she took one of those beer bottles and she smashed it right on the edge of the bar. And we all jumped back . . . and she stood up on top of the bar and she said, 'Hey, watch, everybody—I'm going to do the Dutch Act . . .' and I tried to get her down but she fought me off with the bottle, and everybody was scared the way she was jabbing out at all of us with the bottle, and then she just went for her throat, and then her wrists, and, Christ, she was bleeding and swaying and the bar was all wet from the beer where she spilled it when she broke the bottle and she slipped, and Christ, she fell on the bottle! Man, she fell right on the bottle. The cops came right away but there was nothing nobody could really do and about an hour after they got her to the hospital, well, she was dead. . . ."

Her father came from Minneapolis with his wife, and John Brady, Jr., showed up with the agent and the agent's wife. We wired Timon.

Her father asked us whether or not she had had the last rites. We explained that she had never told anyone she was Catholic so nobody had thought to see that they had been administered. He wanted her body to be buried in a Catholic cemetery, and of course, that was a mess because she was a suicide and they wouldn't bury her in hallowed ground. Her father asked me if I, being a teacher, thought there was something inherited from her mother that had made her do this, and I said I taught English and not Psychology, so he asked Mike and Mike told him that he was just a painter and a friend, to ask her husband, and Brady said that he wasn't making any statements to anybody, to talk to his agent, and the agent said, "Probably."

She had made a will leaving everything to Maude and requesting that she be cremated.

Her father was furious that she had left everything to a maid, and was equally furious about the request for cremation. He asked how such a young person could think of such a thing, and we told him for the same reason such a young person could do such a thing. . . .

And we wondered how a Catholic could leave his wife and remarry, and still find a source of solace in the church.

We bought the coffin you have to buy in order to have a body cremated, and we took it to a crematorium in New Jersey.

Her father didn't want the ashes, and neither did any of the rest of us, so we left them there, and bought the niche for the urn in which the last remains remain.

After it was all over I got in touch with the young colored boy and asked him if he remembered what she had been singing just before she broke the bottle, and he said, "She didn't sing nothing. She just stood on the bar and said this funny poem about being twenty-two."

And I know what she had said. She had said,

·   ·   ·

"When I was one-and-twenty
I heard a wise man say,
'Give crowns and pounds and guineas
But not your heart away;
Give pearls away and rubies
But keep your fancy free.'
But I was one-and-twenty
No use to talk to me.

"When I was one-and-twenty
I heard him say again,
'The heart out of the bosom
Is never given in vain;
'Tis paid with sighs a-plenty
And sold for endless rue.'

"And now I'm two-and-twenty
And it's true, my friends, it's true."

She used to say it just that way. She never got the lyrics right.

About the Author

"The wood sprite who can write"—that's what a national magazine called Audrey Gellen Maas when, at twenty-five, she was a prize-winning editor, producer, and adapter for television. Born on December 7, 1936, and raised in Nyack, New York, she attended Cornell for two years and graduated from Barnard with Honors in Engglish and an award for creative writing.

She started in television as a secretary at Talent Associates, where she soon became a producer and adapter. It was the heyday of the great classics revival, and among the shows she did were *Billy Budd*, *A Tale of Two Cities*, *The Moon and Sixpence*, *The Picture of Dorian Gray*, *The Member of the Wedding*, and *The Power and the Glory*.

She left television to begin *Wait Till the Sun Shines, Nellie*. It took her seven weeks to write the first draft, and as she says, "another year and a half to finish the real Nell." Now at work on her second novel, she lives in New York City and is married to journalist Peter Maas.